Stranger Danger
Lucy McGuffin, Psychic Amateur Detective   Book 4

Maggie March

D1521776

Chihuahua Publishing

Contents

Chapter One

IT'S BEEN THREE DAYS since my best friend Will Cunningham kissed me, then turned right around and lied to my face. Three days and I haven't said squat to anyone. Not about the lie. And most certainly not about the kiss. I'm ready to explode. Worse, I'm ready to confess everything to my older brother, Sebastian, who, luckily, or unluckily, happens to be a Catholic priest.

I drive to the office at St. Perpetua's, where my brother is pastor. Paco, that's my little rescue dog, and I walk through the door where I'm greeted by Shirley Dombrowski, the church secretary. "Hi, Lucy." She stops typing and bends over to scratch Paco behind the ears. He shows his appreciation by wagging his tail. "Aren't you the cutest?" she coos.

Paco looks back at me as if to say, *Doesn't Shirley have good taste?*

Paco is a tan Chihuahua terrier mix with a talent for discovering dead people. Before he came to live with me, his name was Cornelius. His former owner set up a Facebook page for him, and he has, like, a gazillion followers, so he's kind of famous among the woo-woo crowd. The Sunshine Ghost Society, a local group that claims to commune with the dead, has been after me to allow Paco to participate in a séance. I told them I'd think about it.

Which means no.

I know it's selfish of me, but I can't help it. What if something happens to him during the séance? Some rogue ghost could decide to take over his body, which sounds dramatic, but you never know.

"I don't think Father McGuffin is expecting you," says Shirley.

"No worries. I'll just be a minute." I go to walk past her, but Shirley jumps up from her chair and blocks me like she's trying out for a position in the NFL. Pretty impressive considering she had a hip replacement a few months ago. Shirley is in her late sixties and has been widowed for a few years now. She's worked at St. Perpetua's since before I was born and is fiercely loyal to my brother. I thought by now she'd be retired, but Sebastian confided to me once that her late husband left her with a mountain of debt.

"I'm sorry, Lucy, but Father McGuffin left strict instructions that he wasn't to be disturbed. He's working on his Sunday sermon." A sheen of sweat forms on her upper lip. Shirley is either nervous or she's lying.

It just so happens that it's both.

Pretty much anyone would be able to tell that Shirley is nervous. Her demeanor and that glistening upper lip are a sure tell. But the lie about my brother working on his sermon? For the most part, she should have gotten away with it. But I'm not like everyone else. I'm a human lie detector, something that just my family and a handful of friends know about me.

Ever since I was a little girl, I've been able to tell if someone is lying. Call it a gift. Call it a curse. It all depends on your point of view. Lately, it's been more gift than curse because my ability to sniff out deception has helped me solve a few murders around town.

The fact that Shirley is lying about my brother working on his sermon has me more than curious. It seems like such a silly thing to lie about. I absolutely have to know what he's doing.

"Since this is Wednesday, he still has plenty of time," I tell Shirley as Paco and I wiggle past her. Before she can stop me, I fling open the door to my brother's office.

Sebastian looks up from his computer screen and frowns. "Lucy, what are you doing here? Did we have a lunch date?"

Shirley begins sputtering about how she tried to stop me, but my brother puts up a hand to silence her. "No worries," he says, smiling kindly.

She tosses me a disgruntled look before going back to the reception area.

"Don't blame Shirley. She nearly sacrificed her new hip in an attempt to keep me out of here." I flop down on the chair across from the big oak desk where my brother appears to be hard at work. Sebastian is five years older than me, and everyone who's ever seen us together automatically knows that we're brother and sister. We have the same dark, unruly hair, same brown eyes, and same fair skin with freckles. The only difference is I wear glasses and am six inches shorter than him.

Today, he's dressed casually in dark pants and a white shirt and, most importantly, he's minus his collar, which evens out the playing field between us a little. Sure, he's a priest, but right now, I need him to be my older brother.

"Will lied to me," I say. Will Cunningham has been Sebastian's best friend since grade school. When Sebastian went away to the seminary to become a priest, Will slid into my friend zone, except I've been in love with him ever since I was seven. First, he was my brother's best friend, then he became my secret crush, then he became my best friend too.

Sebastian snaps shut his laptop screen. "Oh?" That one simple word reeks of collusion. Sebastian clears his throat in what's clearly a stall tactic. "What did he lie about?"

"I asked Will if he was J.W. Quicksilver."

J.W. Quicksilver is the pen name of a wildly popular author of thriller espionage novels. Everyone in Whispering Bay is crazy about his books, including Betty Jean Collins, the town's bigmouth. Betty Jean runs a weekly book club meeting at her home, and she's going around town bragging to anyone who will listen that she's nabbed J.W. Quicksilver as a guest for her book club meeting tomorrow night.

How Betty Jean was able to convince a national best-selling, highly reclusive author to come to little old Whispering Bay, Florida, for a book club meeting is beyond me. The man is an enigma. He has no photo on his website, and a thorough scan of the Internet produces exactly zip pictures.

I'm ashamed to admit it took me forever to figure out that Will and J.W. Quicksilver were the same person. Will is the head librarian here in town, and he's a huge literary snob. Whenever anyone even mentions the name J.W. Quicksilver, Will starts smirking. It occurred to me a few days ago that maybe Will doth protest too much.

On his days off, Will goes completely offline. Probably because that's when he's writing his novels. Plus, there's the fact that he's been secretly learning how to play pool. I discovered this when we went to visit a pool hall in nearby Panama City. The visit resulted in learning an essential clue that helped me solve a murder, but it also revealed a side to Will I never knew existed. Imagine my shock when I discovered the latest J.W. Quicksilver thriller had a pool shark as a character.

Will tried to brush the whole thing off, telling me that playing pool was his way to relieve tension, but I don't buy it. He was totally doing research for one of his novels.

"Why on earth would you think that Will is J.W. Quicksilver?" Sebastian asks.

Oh boy, the little hairs on the back of my neck start to tickle. Whenever someone lies to me or speaks deceptively, I get a physical reaction. Neck tingles being the most common.

"Well, is he?" I persist.

Sebastian chuckles nervously. "I have work to do—"

"Stop avoiding. Is Will J.W. Quicksilver or not?" Paco barks as if to punctuate my question.

Sebastian looks miserable. "I can't answer that."

And *that* is my answer.

I sit back in my chair, stunned. Even though I knew I was right, now that my brother has basically confirmed it, I'm speechless. But only for a second. "Will is the one who donated the money for the new roof on the church, isn't he? He must be raking in the dough with all those bestselling books of his."

"The church roof came from an anonymous donation. I can't reveal—"

"Yeah, yeah, I get it. I can't believe how blind I've been." My tummy feels like I've eaten too much raw muffin batter. I thought Will and I were best friends. I thought I was important to him. I thought … never mind what I thought. What a chump I've been. "Now that the cat's out of the bag, you can stop playacting."

At the word "cat," Paco sits up in attention. "It's just a matter of speech," I tell my dog. His ears relax, and he slumps back to the ground.

Sebastian sighs heavily. "Can I ask you a question? With your gift, why has it taken you so long to figure it out?"

"Honestly? I'm not sure. Except ... " I hesitate, because this is something I've never told anyone, but what the heck. "I've never been able to catch Will in a lie. Until now."

"Never? But Lucy, he's been lying to you about being J.W. Quicksilver all this time. I don't get it."

"I used to think that the reason I couldn't tell if Will was lying or not was because I kind of have feelings for him, and I thought maybe it messed with my radar."

"Feelings?" Sebastian rolls his head from side to side like he's uncomfortable. "I see."

Poor Sebastian. It must be weird to hear about your best friend and your little sister being linked romantically.

"You never suspected?"

"Not really."

Huh. Neither did Will. Or so he claims. I must be better at hiding my feelings than I thought. I might as well tell Sebastian everything. That is, if Will hasn't told him already.

"The other night at the house during Sunday dinner, Will and I kissed." I study him carefully to gauge his reaction.

"You kissed Will?" Sebastian looks truly surprised. "I thought you and Travis were dating. Isn't that what you told mom and dad?"

Travis Fontaine is the other side of my unexpected love triangle. He's a cop with the Whispering Bay Police force and, if I'm being honest, mighty cute. In a very Ryan Reynolds kind of way. He's also a know-it-all and, despite being shown the evidence, doesn't believe that I'm a lie detector or that Paco is a ghost whisperer, so add extremely stubborn to his resume.

"Correction. Will kissed me. And Travis and I are only fake-dating on account of him covering for me because of my lying to Mom about being a member of Young Catholic Singles."

Sebastian shakes his head at me. "Lucy, you need to get your life together."

Tell me about it.

"If Will is J.W. Quicksilver, then who's this mysterious person going to Betty Jean's book club tomorrow night?" I ask.

"That's the big question."

"Will must be beside himself."

"It's a delicate situation," admits Sebastian. "He can't come out and directly ask Betty Jean too many questions about this impostor without outing himself as the real J.W."

"Poor baby. I feel so sorry for him." I might need a hankie to wipe the sarcasm that's practically dripping from my nose.

"Lucy, he wanted to tell you. He really did."

"So what was stopping him?" Sebastian opens his mouth to say something, but I interrupt, "Never mind. It doesn't matter. There's no reason that's good enough to keep something this big from your supposed best friend. He told you, didn't he?"

"Just don't be too quick to judge until you know the whole story."

"Is that a line from your sermon?"

"What—oh, um, not this week." The guilty look on my brother's face reminds me of Shirley's deception. If Sebastian isn't working on his sermon, what is he working on? And more importantly, why don't he and Shirley want me to see it?

I stand up and stretch my arms over my head, trying to see what's on his desk. All I can make out is a bunch of flyers with the words JOIN US on the top. The rest of the words are hidden beneath a stapler and a bowl of paper clips. Sebastian follows my gaze. His cheeks turn pink.

It's clear he doesn't want me to see what's written on the flyer, which makes me want to see it even more.

"What's that?" I ask, pointing to the flyers.

Sebastian picks up the stack of papers and clutches them against his chest. "Nothing."

Right.

I glance down at Paco, and we lock eyes. I swear, sometimes I think that dog can read my mind because suddenly Paco jumps onto my brother's lap, taking him off guard. The flyers scatter to the floor. I scoop one up. In big letters at the top of the sheet it says, JOIN US TUESDAY NIGHT FOR JESUS AND DOUGHNUTS.

"Lucy—" my brother starts, but it's too late. I've already quickly perused the rest of the flyer.

"You're serving *doughnuts* from Heidi's Bakery at a church social?"

Heidi's Bakery is located in downtown Whispering Bay, just a couple of miles from The Bistro by the Beach, the café I co-own with my friend Sarah Powers. We serve breakfast and lunch and the best muffins you'll ever taste. Not that I would say that about my own muffins, but others have, so who am I to argue?

Recently my café was involved in a reality TV show that pitted six restaurants in our little town against one another for the title of Best Beach Eats. But then Tara Bell, the show's producer, was murdered, and filming shut down, which was a major bummer because I really think The Bistro had a good shot to win. Plus, I could have really used the prize money.

With the help of Paco and my "gift," I was able to solve Tara's murder, but not before making a few enemies around town. Like Heidi Burrows. During a meeting of all the show's participants, I outed her bakery for not disclosing the nutritional values of the food she serves (believe me, if I served food with the crazy calorie and fat counts that she does, I wouldn't disclose it either).

"What's wrong with serving doughnuts from Heidi's?" Sebastian asks defensively. "We always serve doughnuts and coffee after mass in the parish hall. Lucy, you have to get over this irrational jealousy you have of Heidi's Bakery."

"First off, I'm not jealous of Heidi and her overpriced doughnuts. But this isn't mass, and you never serve premium doughnuts from Heidi's. So what is this?" I wave the flyer in his face.

Paco barks as if to say, *Yeah, what is this?*

"It's a one-time program. We're having a speaker come from the diocese, and Heidi offered to provide free refreshments. What was I supposed to do? Turn her down?"

"No, Judas Iscariot, you were supposed to ask your sister. I could have comped the muffins. Which, by the way, are lots healthier than doughnuts. First Will, now you." I look at Paco. "C'mon, boy, at least you're still loyal to me."

Paco lifts his chin in the air, then turns his back on Sebastian. *Good dog.*

My brother frowns. "Don't you think you're blowing this out of proportion?"

"I hope you're current on your CPR because those doughnuts of Heidi's are loaded with enough fat to give the entire congregation a heart attack."

"Lucy—" he pleads.

But I don't hear the rest of what he's saying because I'm already out the door with Paco on my heels. I sit in my car, too agitated to turn on the ignition.

My best friend has been lying to me for years, and my brother is in cahoots with the enemy (aka Heidi). And if that wasn't enough, some ... con man is running around impersonating J.W. Quicksilver, for what reasons, no one knows. I'm fake-dating the new cop in town, and if my mother finds out I've been lying to her about it, she'll make me join Young Catholic Singles. Well, technically, since I'm twenty-six and financially independent, she can't make me do anything, but she'll guilt me into joining because I don't have the guts to stand up to her.

My brother is right. My life is a mess.

Chapter Two

I GET BACK TO The Bistro by the Beach just in time to help with the last-minute lunch crowd. "Thanks for letting me sneak out for a few minutes," I tell Sarah.

"No problem." Sarah is a few years older than me, blonde, blue-eyed, gorgeous, calm, cool, and collected. She also makes the best macaroni and cheese you've ever tasted. Her husband, Luke, owns an environmental engineering firm and does quite well for himself. Besides being my business partner, she's a good friend and my role model. When I grow up, I want to be just like her. Something I'm not doing a very good job with, considering how I stormed out of my brother's office.

The last customer in line picks up his order. "What did you need to talk to Sebastian about? Or is it none of my business?" asks Sarah.

Since Sebastian was a bust, I might as well confide in her. Which is probably what I should have done from the beginning. Sarah is one of the few people who know both about my gift and about my feelings for Will. She's been after me to come clean with him for some time now.

"You'll be happy to know that Will and I finally had the *talk*."

Her mouth hangs open for a second, then snaps back shut. "And?"

"And he said he felt the same way. Then he kissed me."

She squeals, which draws the attention of a few of our seated customers, as well as Paco, who looks up at me from his place behind the counter. "Was it fabulous?"

"The kiss? I mean, sure, it was great."

"Great?" She makes a face. "Girl, I want to hear that you saw fireworks and ... oh, does this mean you liked Travis's kiss better?"

Travis Fontaine, my fake boyfriend, kissed me a couple of weeks ago. He wants us to date for real but not until I sort out my feelings for Will.

"It's not a case of better. They were just ... different." Even though I don't have a lot of experience in this department, both kisses were pretty good. I thought that once I kissed Will, any feelings I had for Travis would disappear, but that isn't the case, which means I'm still confused. "Right after Will kissed me, he lied to me."

Sarah's eyes widen. "What about?"

I wince. "Sorry, I can't tell you. It's complicated."

"It's probably better that I don't know, but Lucy, what are you going to do about Travis and Will?"

"I have no idea."

She mulls this over a few seconds. "I was thinking, I know how much you hate owing Will money. That sort of thing always mucks up a relationship, so if it makes things easier, I could cover the loan. That way you'd owe me and not Will."

When Sarah and I bought The Bistro earlier this year, I was ten thousand dollars short on my half of the down payment to qualify for the bank loan, so Will lent it to me. I've been trying like crazy to pay him back, but between my culinary school student loans and Paco's vet bill when he was poisoned by a crazy killer (that's another story), I haven't been able to come up with the dough. Will told me he was in no hurry to get paid back. At first, I was skeptical, because how much could he save as a small-town librarian? Now that I know he's a world-famous author who goes around donating church roofs without blinking an eye, it makes sense. But Sarah is right. I want to pay him that money back ASAP because it doesn't feel right between us until I do.

"That's awful sweet of you, but it's a lot of money. I already have the benefit of a free apartment." The Bistro's previous owners lived above the café in a two-bedroom, one-thousand-square-foot apartment that they renovated shortly before selling to us. Since Sarah's husband, Luke, already had a house on the beach, they had no interest in moving here, so it only made sense that I'd be the one to get the apartment.

"And I have a husband who makes a lot of money," says Sarah. "Besides, I saved up more for this place than what I ended up using, so it's not a problem. Just say the word."

This is tempting. And yeah, owing Sarah is better than owing Will, especially since she and I are already business partners. Ideally, though, I wouldn't owe anyone money. Except the bank. We'll be paying the mortgage on this place until we're gray.

"I don't know how long it might take me to pay you back in full."

"No worries," she says. "I actually have a few ideas about that."

Before I can ask her what those ideas might be, the door to The Bistro opens, and Betty Jean Collins walks in, followed by Brittany Kelly. Brittany is the PR person for the chamber of commerce and my former nemesis. We went to high school together, but we were never friends until recently. Sometimes she can be a royal pain in my gluteus maximus, but she has some great qualities. She's feisty and loyal, and if you're ever being held hostage by a madman, you can totally count on her. The only problem is she's got a crush on Will. In her defense, she has no idea how I feel about him, which complicates things to no end.

"Well, hello, Lucy." Betty Jean saunters to the counter with the most self-satisfied smile I've ever seen, which is saying a lot because she generally walks around town like she owns the place.

Betty Jean is eighty, but she's not the kind of eighty-year-old who shows you pictures of her grandchildren and offers to make you chicken noodle soup when you get sick. She's originally from Boston and has been married and divorced four times. There are three things Betty Jean loves most in the world: the Red Sox. Prepping for any kind of natural disaster. And younger men. She's a prominent member of the Gray Flamingos, a local senior citizens activist group, and if she feels like she's been slighted in any way, no one at the AARP is getting any rest until the issue has been resolved.

"Aren't you excited about my book club meeting tomorrow night?" she asks. "I told you I'd get J.W. Quicksilver."

I wonder just how smug Betty Jean would be if she knew that whoever she has coming to her book club meeting is nothing but a big fat impostor. I should warn her, but I can't do that without exposing Will.

"Well—"

"Oh, c'mon, Lucy. Say it. You didn't think I could get him here, did you?" she crows, only there's something off about her expression. It's like that smirk has been frozen on her face.

"Betty Jean, did you get Botox?"

She lifts her chin in the air and turns her face from side to side. "I look twenty years younger, don't I?"

"Well ... sure. Whatever you say. Um, so I take it you've met this J.W. in person?"

"Not yet," admits Betty Jean. "But I've spoken to him over the phone." She exchanges a sly look with Brittany.

"I've spoken to him too." Brittany giggles like she and Betty Jean share a secret joke. How irritating.

"And?" I ask impatiently.

"Tonight, all will be revealed," Betty Jean says mysteriously.

"What will be revealed?"

"The reason why J.W. Quicksilver is such a recluse. And that's all I'll say on the matter."

"Are you sure I can't torture it out of you?" I ask, only half-joking.

"My lips are sealed. Let me just say that you won't be disappointed."

Her lips aren't exactly sealed, but the Botox is making them—wait. "Why will all be revealed tonight? I thought the book club meeting was tomorrow."

"Oh, it is," says Brittany, "but that's what we came to tell you. I've arranged for J.W. to do a reading and a private signing tonight."

Private signing? "I don't understand. When did all this happen?"

"After J.W. got in touch with Betty Jean, she gave me his information and I was able to put together this fabulous event at Daddy's restaurant. It sold out in less than an hour, but that was to be expected since J.W. is a literary genius."

"I thought you didn't like his books." Just the other night at my parents' house, Brittany was dogging on the latest J.W Quicksilver novel. I think she was doing it to score points with Will, who openly disdains anything the man writes. If only Brittany knew the truth.

She flushes. "Did I say that? You must have heard wrong because I love his books! He'll be doing a reading, and there will be hors d'oeuvres and champagne. It's like nothing Whispering Bay has ever seen before. It's a huge PR coup for me ... I mean, for the town. Once word spreads that J.W. Quicksilver has come to Whispering Bay, then I expect other big-name authors to follow."

"I've already extended an invitation to Lee Child," says Betty Jean. "Hopefully, I'll hear from him soon."

"I just hope Lee Child gives us more advance notice than J.W . Quicksilver," says Brittany. "Do you know how hard it is to plan an event like the one at Daddy's restaurant in less than twenty-four hours? Good thing I have all those years of experience putting together sorority mixers."

"Lee Child?" I sputter. "As in *the* Lee Child who writes the Jack Reacher books?"

Betty Jean looks amused. "If I can get J.W. Quicksilver, why can't I get Lee Child?"

I take a deep breath and try to reason with her. "Betty Jean, have you asked yourself why a highly popular reclusive author that no one has ever seen before is going to come out to the world here in Whispering Bay, Florida? Why isn't he making his first public appearance on *Good Morning America* or on *Oprah*?"

"Honestly, Lucy, my book club has much more clout than you're giving it credit for. Do you know that I've had to turn down a dozen people wanting to join just in the past few days? Besides, Oprah only picks books that no one reads on their own. J.W. doesn't need her endorsement."

"Plus, I'm pretty sure Oprah doesn't have a show anymore," adds Brittany.

I fight the urge to roll my eyes. "I was just using that as an example."

"Let's not argue about how all this happened," says Brittany. "The important thing is that J.W.'s visit will make Whispering Bay the new literary capital of the Southeast." She reaches out and gives Betty Jean a hug. "And we owe it all to Betty Jean and her persistence!"

The only explanation I can come up with is that the Botox has seeped into Betty Jean's brain and spilled over into Brittany's as well.

Brittany looks at me and frowns. "What's wrong, Lucy? You don't look happy. Just think of what all this could potentially mean for The Bistro. All that tourist money! I'm thinking of setting up a book festival next spring. What do you think? Or maybe we should do it in the winter, when all the snowbirds are here."

This is going too far. I don't want to give Will away, but I can't let the entire town make fools of themselves. "Look, there's something important I need to tell you—"

"Is this pouty face because you think you're going to miss out on tonight's big event?" asks Brittany. "No way was I going to let that happen to my best friend! I was going to set aside a ticket for you, but Travis took care of it."

I still. "What does Travis Fontaine have to do with this?"

"He's your boyfriend, silly. Who else would you go with? I stopped by the police station to arrange security for tonight, and when he found out about the event, he immediately bought two tickets." She blinks. "Shoot. Maybe I wasn't supposed to say anything. Maybe he wants it to be a surprise."

Betty Jean checks her watch. "Considering it starts in four hours, he'd better unsurprise her fast."

"What are you going to wear?" asks Brittany.

"Since I just found out about this, I have no idea."

"It's not fancy, but it is cocktail attire, so don't wear your sneakers. Or any of those T-shirts with those goofy sayings."

I glance down at my shirt, which says MUCH ADO ABOUT MUFFIN. "What's wrong with my shirt?"

"Nothing, if you're trying to get a date with the Pillsbury Dough Boy, but you've managed to snag Whispering Bay's newest eligible bachelor. You need to wear something sexy."

Betty Jean manages to break through the Botox to snort. "Lucy? Sexy? Let's not ask for miracles." She gives me a thorough look-over. "How she managed to get that hottie Travis Fontaine interested in her is beyond me."

"I'll tell you how Lucy snagged Travis," says Brittany. "Not only is she pretty and smart and makes the best muffins in the world, she's wonderfully witty. That's how."

Wow. "Gosh, Brittany, I'm really touched."

"Wear a dress. Better yet, text me a picture of what you plan to wear so I can approve it."

Right. "So, by any chance, do you know if Will got a ticket?" I ask.

Brittany beams. "As a matter of fact, I just asked him to go with me, and he said yes."

Oh, he did, did he?

Betty Jean taps her watch. "That's enough chitchat. We need to go make sure everything is set up perfectly for tonight. Oh, and Lucy, don't forget you're making the muffins for the book club meeting tomorrow night."

Rats. I'd forgotten about that. The situation is getting stickier by the minute. First, there's this reading tonight, then the book club meeting. Will absolutely has to tell everyone the truth. But until he does, I need to play along. "Sure, I'll bring muffins. What kind do you want?"

"Your best, naturally. And don't try to pawn off any of your left-overs either. They have to be fresh. We can't have a world-renowned celebrity like J.W. Quicksilver eating day-old muffins."

I slap my hand over my forehead like I'm about to faint. "Goodness, no. We couldn't allow a day-old muffin to pass through J.W.'s sacred lips. The entire literary world might collapse."

Betty Jean tries to narrow her eyes at me (at least I think that's what she's doing). "If it's too much of an imposition to provide the muffins, just let me know. Heidi offered me freshly made doughnuts. Lots of them. I can call her if—"

"I'll make the muffins."

"That's what I thought you'd say. Have them at the house no later than six. And wear your work apron."

"I thought the book club meeting started at seven." *Wait.* Why would she want me to wear my apron, unless ... "Betty Jean, are you expecting me to act as a server during your meeting?"

She sniffs. "You did miss the last meeting you were invited to. Consider yourself a probationary member of the club. You can serve during this meeting, and if you don't mess anything up, you can come to the next meeting as a regular member."

Of all the ... I can practically feel the steam coming out of my ears. "I missed the last meeting because I found a dead body in the park. Remember?"

"So you say. Really, Lucy, if you don't want to do it, just say the word and I'll call Heidi."

Unbelievable. I wish I could tell Betty Jean where she could stuff my muffins, but instead I force a smile. "Fresh-baked muffins at six. Me and my apron will be there."

"I'm glad that's settled." She snaps her fingers at Brittany. "Let's go."

"Bye, Lucy!" Brittany yells on her way out. "Don't forget, text me a picture of your outfit!"

I turn to Sarah. "Did you know about this big shindig at The Harbor House tonight?"

Sarah nods. "The customers have been talking about it. Apparently, it's easier to get *Hamilton* tickets on Broadway than it is to this reading tonight."

I bite my tongue. I wish I could tell Sarah how this big event is nothing but a ruse. I can't put this off any longer. Will has got to set this whole thing straight. I pull off my apron. "I know I ducked out earlier, but I really have to talk to someone, and it can't wait."

"Will?" she asks with a knowing smile. "We're about to close anyway. I'll do final cleanup."

I hug her. "Thanks. I owe you one."

"Are you really going to text Brittany a picture of your outfit for her approval?" Sarah asks.

"If I don't, I'll never hear the end of it." It occurs to me that maybe I can have a little fun with this. Brittany wants sexy? I'll give her sexy. "I think I have just the outfit."

Chapter Three

THE WHISPERING BAY PUBLIC Library is located next to the police station and the municipal building adjacent to the crystal-clear blue waters of the Gulf of Mexico. It's early December, and the weather in north Florida is heavenly. Blue skies, low humidity, sixty-eight degrees. Only I can't appreciate how beautiful it is because all I can think about is what a big mess Will has gotten himself and the rest of the town into.

Since Paco is staying in the car, I leave the windows rolled down. "No barking, understand? Unless you see a squirrel. Then you have my full permission to go crazy." Paco pants like he agrees. I suffer from sciurophobia, so anything to take the little demons down a peg or two is fine in my book.

I go to the front desk and ask Faith, one of the librarians, if Will is in his office.

"He went home early. Lucky dog. He got a ticket to tonight's big event at The Harbor House to see J. W. Quicksilver. Ironic, huh? Will doesn't like any of his books, and I'd give anything to hear the man talk. And to see him." She leans across the counter and lowers her voice. "I wonder if he's as sexy in real life as his books."

Ironic is the word of the day, all right. I wonder how Faith would react if I told her that she sees J.W. Quicksilver every day at work.

It hits me then just how much Will's life is going to change after everyone discovers who he really is. Is he going to keep his job at the library? Sure, as a city employee he has good benefits, but that hardly outweighs the advantages of being able to write full-time. I imagine he'll probably quit his job. What if he leaves town? Will's parents are divorced. His mom lives in Miami, and his dad is up in Chicago. He could decide to move closer to one of them. Or he could move to New York and live in a loft overlooking Central Park while he drinks lattes and writes all day. He could do anything he wants. There's nothing keeping him here in boring old Whispering Bay.

I try to imagine what my life would be like if Will moved away. No more Friday nights sitting on the couch eating Tiny's pizza and watching *America's Most Vicious Criminals* while arguing over who did it or if the police are going after the wrong suspect. No more laughing over the table at my parents' house during Sunday night dinners. No more listening to him rant about how all everyone wants now is the instant gratification of watching the movie over reading the book.

A world without Will feels ... empty.

I say goodbye to Faith and head back outside to my car, where Paco has been waiting patiently. We drive to Will's, but before I can knock, he opens the door. "I saw you pull up." He looks down at Paco. "Hey, boy."

Normally, Paco is all over Will, begging for every little scrap of attention he can get, but not today. He trots right by Will like he's never seen him before.

Will looks hurt. "What's up with the pooch?"

"Oh, I don't know. He's pretty good at reading people. Maybe he doesn't trust you anymore."

"Lucy—"

"I hear you're going to see J.W. Quicksilver at The Harbor House tonight. Funny. I didn't think you liked his books." I sit down on the couch, calmly cross my arms over my chest, waiting.

"Let me explain," he begins.

"By all means."

He sits in the chair across from me. "So ... " He blows out a breath. "I guess you figured out that I'm ... " He shakes his head like he can't bring himself to say it.

"What? That you're J.W. Quicksilver? Yeah. It took me a while, but I finally got it. What I don't get is why you never told me. Or why you lied to me when I asked you the other day. Right after kissing me, I might add."

"It's complicated."

Huh. That's exactly what I said to Sarah.

"The kiss or the lie?" I ask.

"Both," he says miserably. "Crap." He rakes a hand through his dark hair. "That didn't come out right. It's the lie that's complicated. Not the kiss. The kiss was great."

This seems like the perfect opening to talk about where our relationship is headed, but I can't think about that until we clear up the mess he's made with this J.W. Quicksilver business.

"What do you know about this faker who's pretending to be you?" I ask.

"Not much except that he approached Betty Jean after she posted on an online review site. He must be trolling reader sites and preying on the clueless."

"But what does he possibly hope to gain from this?"

"Besides getting his jollies impersonating me? I have no idea. All I know is that this is really bad."

"I agree." I think back to how excited Betty Jean and Brittany were when they came into the café. "You know Betty Jean got Botox in anticipation of meeting you?"

Will looks horrified. And he hasn't even seen Betty Jean try to smile yet.

"You have to fix this. You have to tell everyone that you're the real J.W. Quicksilver."

"That's what Sebastian says I should do." He puts his head between his hands. "I wanted to come out on my own terms. Not like this."

"You write popular thrillers. Big deal. Who else knows that you're the real J.W.? Besides Sebastian?"

"Just my publisher. And my agent. And now you."

"Not even your parents?"

Will shakes his head. Wait ... Will has an agent? It reminds me once again of the secret life he's been living, and I can't help but feel resentful.

"The way I see it, you don't have a choice. You either out this impostor or you let him go around being you. By the way, I hear you're going to the reading tonight with Brittany."

He looks at me. "It's not a date."

"Does Brittany know that?"

"As a matter of fact, she does."

I still. "Oh."

"I told her I wanted to be friends. That's all. The tickets were sold out, so it was the only way I could go."

Speaking of which, I really need to secure my own ticket to this circus. "Hold on a sec." I pull out my cell phone and text Travis.

Hey. I heard through Brittany that you have an extra ticket to the J.W. Quicksilver event tonight. Any chance I can use it?

He texts back almost immediately. **It depends on how nicely you ask**.

I fight back the urge to put him in his place. **Can I please have your extra ticket**?

He makes me sweat a couple of minutes before he responds.

Lucy, are you asking me out on a date? Because if you are, then the answer is yes.

No, you big headed egomaniac, I'm not asking you out on a date. Before I hit send on this, I reconsider. It's probably not the best response if I want to get that extra ticket. I reluctantly delete it. **Sure, whatever**, I text instead.

You don't sound very excited. I don't know. This ticket seems to be in high demand. Maybe I should hold out for someone who really wants it.

What he means is that he's in high demand. A single good-looking man in this town is more popular than a hero in a Jane Austen novel. Apparently, the only way I'm going to get this ticket is to grovel. I grit my teeth. **I would love to go on a date with you**.

That's better. I'll pick you up at six thirty.

Ack. I feel so dirty. I toss my cell phone back in my bag. "Okay, so I have a ticket to tonight's event too."

"With Fontaine?"

"Yep."

Will frowns. "Does he know that you and I are together now?"

"News flash. You and I are most certainly not together." If you'd told me just a week ago that I'd be saying that to Will, I'd have thought you were crazy. He starts to say something, but I stop him. "Right now, we have more important stuff to fix than our relationship. So, what's it going to be? Are you going to tell everyone that you're J.W. Quicksilver or not?"

"You're right," he says grimly. "I don't have a choice."

I nod, relieved that he's finally gotten it through his thick skull that he needs to own up to this. "So how are you going to do it?"

He shrugs. "I'm not sure. What do you think?"

"What I think is that it never should have come to this, but since it has, it's the perfect opportunity to come out. Everyone who's bought a ticket is coming to see J.W. Quicksilver, right? So just march up in front of the room and tell everyone the truth."

"You don't think they'll be upset with me?"

"Upset? They'll be thrilled. J.W. Quicksilver, an international best-selling author living right here under their noses this whole time? Believe me, the whole town is going to be talking about this for a long time to come."

Lucy, you absolutely can NOT wear that.

I read Brittany's text and giggle.

I put together the most absurd outfit I could rummage from my closet—a too-tight latex miniskirt that I think I wore back in the eighth grade, fishnet hose (leftovers from a Halloween costume) and a sports bra. Then I took a selfie and sent it to Brittany, asking her opinion.

I know it's bad of me, but honestly, after the crack she made about my T-shirts, she kind of deserves it.

Why can't I wear this? I text back. **You and Betty Jean told me to try and look sexy. Don't I look nice**?

Lucy, please, I BEG of you. Take it off. Put on anything else but this.

Anything?

Yes, anything!

Oh, goody! I've been wanting to show off my new T-shirt. The caption reads: I LIKE BIG MUFFINS AND I CANNOT LIE.

I wait for her response, but nothing comes. Knowing Brittany, she's contemplating how much time it will take her to dash over here to perform a rescue mission on my outfit. A few minutes later, I get a weak smiley face from her and a text that reads **Sounds good**.

I'm about to text and tell her that I'm messing with her when there's a knock on my back door. Uh-oh. Travis. I was having so much fun with this that I forgot the time.

I take a quick look in the mirror to make sure I'm put together. Knee-length black velvet dress. Heels. Red lipstick. My hair is scooped up into a messy bun (it took me two hours to get it looking this good and messy), and I'm wearing contacts instead of glasses. I'm channeling my inner Anne Hathaway from the movie *The Devil Wears Prada*. Not the before look when she's all frumpy and sad-looking. I'm aiming for the after look when the Stanley Tucci character takes pity on her and gives her a makeover.

I bought this dress a year ago on a whim, but I've been too chicken to wear it until now. It would probably hang in my closet until the moths ate it up, except Betty Jean dared me to look sexy, and I'm not one to back down from a challenge, especially when she's the one issuing it. This irrational need to always have the last word or always be right is a huge character flaw of mine. I wish I could brush things off as easily as Sarah does. What do I care that Heidi's Bakery is catering the church social? Or if she provides the refreshments for Betty Jean's book club?

Except I do. Muffins are always getting the short end of the stick. Sure, anyone can whip up a pretentious cupcake or a greasy doughnut, but making a really good muffin is an art form.

I swirl around to get Paco's opinion. "What do you think? And be honest. Do I look good, or do I look like a clown?"

Paco wags his tail and barks in excitement.

I probably shouldn't have worded it that way.

"Let's try again. One bark for I look good, two barks for I look like a clown." I hold my breath and wait.

Paco barks one time, then dances around in a circle.

Well, there you go. My dog thinks I look good.

That settles that.

I grab my purse and a light sweater and head down the stairs to the café, where Travis Fontaine is waiting on my back doorstep. I've seen Travis in his police uniform, of course, and jeans and casual slacks, but I've never seen him in a suit. He's wearing black pants and a matching blazer with a light blue dress shirt open at the collar. He also smells terrific.

"Holy *wow*. You look good enough to---" I snap my mouth shut before I say something I know I'll regret.

"To eat?" he finishes with a knowing grin.

I wish I could dissemble better, but I'm no good at hiding what I think.

"Okay, so you look good. Big deal."

His smile fades as he takes in my outfit. "And you look fantastic. Really, Lucy. Great dress."

My cheeks go hot. "Thanks."

Paco looks between the two of us and wags his tail. Travis scores points by reaching down and scratching him in his favorite spot behind the ear. "Hey, little guy, I'm taking Lucy out tonight. You okay with that?"

Paco barks as if to say, *Yes*!

"Be a good boy," I tell my dog, "and if you find any dead people, call 911." I add this last part as a dig to Travis.

He chuckles. "You still think your dog sees ghosts?"

Under Travis's eagle eye, I make sure to lock my door. He's always after me about security, something I have to admit to being lax on in the past. But ever since I found my first dead body, I'm more than happy to oblige. "I don't *think* Paco sees ghosts. I know he does."

"And you're a human lie detector," he adds, shaking his head in disbelief.

When Tara Bell was found murdered in my kitchen, I had no choice but to tell Travis the truth about me and Paco. I thought that once he knew about our special skills, he'd let me assist with the police investigation, but he didn't believe me. He thinks I'm "intuitive" and that Paco, whose history before I rescued him is a bit sketchy, has been trained as a cadaver dog.

How many chihuahua terrier mixes do you know that serve as cadaver dogs? None. That's how many. But Travis is too stubborn to open his mind to the truth.

"One day you'll feel foolish for doubting me."

He raises a brow as if to say he'll take his chances on that.

"So, about tonight," I begin.

"What about tonight?"

"Thanks for getting tickets. I had no idea you were a J.W. Quicksilver fan."

"I'm not," he says, "but I know how much you like his books."

I start to open my car door, but he beats me to the punch. I've been in a car with Travis before, but he's never been this chivalrous. I go over the evidence in my head.

1. Nice suit.

2. Cologne.

3. Opens the car door for me.

4. Bought tickets for tonight because of me.

If I didn't know any better, I'd think this is a real date.

"Thanks," I say cautiously.

"My pleasure." He smiles, and my insides go all mushy.

Oh no. My girl parts think this is a real date too.

Chapter Four

THE HARBOR HOUSE IS owned by Brittany's family and is Whispering Bay's fanciest eatery, serving premium seafood and upscale cocktails. I worked here during the summers while I was in high school. Even though the work was hard, the experience cemented my passion for cooking.

The parking lot is crammed with cars, and the valets are directing everyone to an overflow lot. Rusty Newton, a local cop and one of my favorite customers (he comes by every morning for a cup of coffee and a lemon poppy seed muffin), is assisting with traffic flow. Rusty is what the locals call a good old boy. He's in his mid-forties, and he's been on the force forever. He and the department's receptionist, Cindy, have been dating for a while now.

Seeing a police presence at the event reminds me that Whispering Bay's finest might be needed before the night is out. Impersonating another person has to be a crime, right?

"Do you know if Rusty is going to be here all night?" I ask Travis.

"Why?"

"Just wondering. So ... could you arrest someone if you had to? I mean, since you're not on duty?"

"Why? Are you expecting a rumble?" he teases. "Some overzealous fans planning to rush the stage and fight one another to get the first autograph?"

"Not exactly."

The humor in his eyes fades. "Lucy, do you know something I don't?"

I wish I could give Travis the heads-up on what's about to go down, but I promised Will he could do this his way. I clamp my mouth shut before I accidentally spill the beans.

Travis groans. "Promise me you're not planning some kind of crazy shenanigans tonight."

"What on earth makes you think that?"

He raises a brow.

"Okay, so maybe in the past, I've pulled a few stunts, but it was always for a good cause. Like finding a killer," I remind him. "But there's no unsolved murder, no dead bodies, nothing to worry about. Right?"

"Right," he says, but he doesn't sound confident. Considering our history, I can't blame him.

We leave his car with a valet. Inside the building, we're shown to a private salon with a terrific view of the gulf. The room holds maybe two hundred people, and it's packed. Brittany is right. This event is big. I glance around to see lots of familiar faces, including—

"Lucy!" My mother scurries across the room to give me a hug. She's got a glass of champagne in one hand and a yummy-looking appetizer in the other. "Isn't this exciting! J.W. Quicksilver here in Whispering Bay!" She steps back to get a look at Travis and me. "Well, don't you two look wonderful! Is that a new dress?"

"Um, sort of."

My father, who's always three steps behind my mother, catches up to the conversation. "Hello, kids," he says good-naturedly.

Travis shakes Dad's hand. "George. Good to see you again." He gives my mother a smile straight out of the Eddie Haskell school of smarm. "Molly, you look lovely. You and Lucy could be sisters."

Mom titters like a schoolgirl. "Aren't you the charmer?"

Oh, brother. "I didn't know you two would be here tonight."

"Why wouldn't we?" says Mom. "After all, we're part of Betty Jean's book club. She gave us all a heads-up so we were sure to get tickets."

"Practically the whole town's here," says Dad. He waves across the room to Victor Marino, who's chatting it up with Phoebe Van Cleave. They're both members of the Sunshine Ghost Society and the principal naggers who want to involve Paco in a séance. Victor waves back. Besides them, I recognize lots of my regular customers, as well as most members of the Gray Flamingos.

"I had no idea this room could hold so many people," says Mom. "Makes it the perfect place for a wedding reception, doesn't it?" She winks at Travis.

I wish the floor would swallow me whole. Thankfully, before Mom can book the band for my nonexistent reception, Dad slaps Travis on the back. "Why don't I buy you a real drink while we let the girls gab?"

Travis throws me an amused look as Dad takes him away to the bar.

"Look! Even Will is here," says Mom. "And you know how much he dislikes J.W.'s books. I guess as the town librarian, he felt it was his duty to attend. Don't he and Brittany make just the cutest couple?" I follow Mom's gaze. Brittany looks spectacular in a slim navy-blue dress and heels. Will is wearing a suit, and he looks incredibly handsome. I have to agree with Mom. They do look good together.

A waiter passing out champagne comes our way. I grab a flute off his tray and take a chug. I have a feeling I'm going to need a few more of these to get through the night. "Have you seen J.W. Quicksilver yet?"

"Not yet," says Mom. "But I've met his personal assistant."

"He has a personal assistant?" This is getting stickier by the second.

"Well, of course he does. All the big celebrities have them." Mom points to a woman standing in the middle of a group. Mid-twenties, brown hair pulled back in a bun, glasses, kind of frumpy. "Her name is Anita something. Very nice, but the poor woman looks a bit overwhelmed. Although you'd think she'd be used to all this by now. J.W. is a worldwide sensation. He probably attracts a lot of attention wherever he goes."

Before I can respond, an older woman comes up to join us. She's got long, blonde hair, and her dress is so tight, it's a wonder she can breathe. "Ladies, are you having a good time?" Her voice is oddly familiar. If I didn't know better, I'd think it was—

My champagne goes down the wrong way. "*Betty Jean?*" I sputter. "Is that you?"

Even Mom isn't quite sure what to make of this. "You look ... well, you look ... Betty Jean Collins, how on earth did you get yourself into that dress?"

"It's called Spanx. Don't you think I look like Farrah Fawcett?" She carefully pats her blonde curls. "It's a wig. But don't tell anyone."

"What's up with your face?" asks Mom, making her my new personal hero.

"Botox. And a makeover at the Clinique counter at Dillard's."

"Don't you think that long, blonde hair looks a bit ... too much for a woman your age?" Mom says, trying to be tactful.

Betty Jean makes a huffing sound. "If Christie Brinkley can get away with it, why can't I?"

"For one thing, Christie Brinkley is younger than you," I say. "Plus, you know, she's a supermodel."

"Phooey. The only difference between me and Christie Brinkley, besides a few years, is that she has a really good team behind her. I'm thinking of getting my neck done. What do you think? And be honest."

Before I can give Betty Jean what she's asked for, Mom discreetly elbows me in the ribs. "Whatever makes you happy, dear. Now tell us, because we're dying to know. Have you met J.W. yet?"

"I'll say." Betty Jean makes a growling sound. "And I'm happy to report that he's just as yummy in person as he is on the phone."

Mom leans in. "What's he like?" she asks eagerly.

"Terribly handsome. You can all thank me later."

"Why should we thank you?" I ask.

"Because, Lucy McGuffin," says Betty Jean with attitude, "if it wasn't for me, J.W. wouldn't even know that Whispering Bay exists. If I hadn't reached out to him, tonight would never be happening, so you're all very welcome."

I'm not sure how much more of this foolishness I can stand. Betty Jean does a double take like she's just now noticing my dress. "Yowza. I'm impressed. I didn't think you could pull it off."

"Pull what off?" asks a deep male voice from over my shoulder.

I turn around to see Will. Next to him is Brittany, who practically wilts with relief at the sight of my dress. "Thank goodness you came to your senses," she says.

"Came to her senses about what?" asks Will.

"Betty Jean dared Lucy to look sexy tonight," explains Brittany. "And at first ... well, it doesn't matter. What matters is that she got it right in the end. Did Travis go crazy over your dress?" she asks me.

I feel my face go hot. "He liked it all right."

In what is undoubtedly the most awkward moment of my life thus far, Brittany turns to Will. "Don't you think Lucy looks fabulous?"

Will and I lock eyes in a guilt-ridden gaze. It's not fair to keep my feelings for Will from Brittany, especially when I know how much she likes him. Sure, Will might have told her that he just wants to be friends, but knowing Brittany, she probably doesn't believe him. Once this J.W. Quicksilver business is taken care of, I need to have a long talk with all the parties involved in my messy not-so-love life.

"I always think Lucy looks great," Will says diplomatically.

Travis and Dad come back with drinks in their hands, and everyone starts making small talk.

The lights in the room dim, then flash back on. "That's my cue!" Brittany hands me her champagne glass. "I have to introduce J.W." She makes her way to the front of the room and picks up a mic. "Good evening, y'all!" It's amazing how Brittany's Southern accent goes up two notches whenever she's in front of an audience. "If y'all wouldn't mind taking your seats, it's time for our program to begin."

I hurry to get the best seat possible in the front row. Travis sits on my right, and Shirley Dombrowski takes a seat on my left. I lean over and whisper, "I didn't know you were a J.W. Quicksilver fan."

Shirley's cheeks pinken. "Don't tell Father, but I've read chapter fifteen from Assassin's Creed four times now!"

"We all have," I mutter.

I crane my neck and spot Will seated next to my parents a few rows over. Mom and Dad look practically giddy, while Will's expression remains grim. The air around us is thick with excitement. My heart thumps with anticipation. I can't wait until Will tells everyone the truth. People will be shocked, yes, but they'll also be excited when they realize we have an honest-to-goodness celebrity living right here in town.

Brittany begins her introduction, reading off a list of J.W. Quicksilver's literary accomplishments. So far, everything is straight out of his website bio. "One more thing," she adds, her voice turning stern. "As you're all aware, Mr. Quicksilver is a very private person. Absolutely no photography is allowed tonight." Brittany lets everyone absorb this a minute. "It's now my great pleasure to give you the one and only bestselling author Mr. J.W. Quicksilver!"

The room erupts with applause. A man in his early sixties emerges from a side door and walks up to the podium. Tall, with silver hair and a neatly trimmed beard, he's wearing a waist-length black jacket with a bowtie and a green plaid kilt.

What? A kilt?

He flashes us a roguish smile. "Good evening, Whispering Bay," he says in a deliciously deep Scottish brogue. "It's a pleasure to be here."

Shirley gasps, then clutches my hand. "Oh my God. It's Sean Connery!"

While the rest of the crowd is taking in the fact that J.W. is apparently Scottish, I give this faker a thorough perusal. No, not Sean Connery, but close enough. Movie star good looks and a Scottish accent. This guy is good. No wonder Betty Jean is running around town making a fool of herself.

I try to catch Will's attention, but like the rest of the crowd, he's riveted by this fake, who begins reading a passage from the latest book in the series, *Assassin's Revenge*. I've read the book, so none of this is new to me, but *holy wow*, this guy with his deep Highland brogue is putting a whole new spin on things. He looks up occasionally to make eye contact with the audience. His gaze drifts slowly until it reaches my row. We lock eyes. Then he winks at me. *The nerve.*

Shirley sucks in a breath. "Lucy, J.W. Quicksilver just winked at me!" She nearly squeezes the life from my hand. "Do you think he's wearing anything under his kilt?"

"Shirley, for Pete's sake, control yourself." I disentangle my hand from her grasp.

"Sorry, I'm just so overwhelmed."

I'll say. Poor Shirley. I don't want to burst her bubble and tell her that he was winking at me and not her. At least, I think it was me.

I glance around the room. Nearly every woman appears to be mesmerized by this fake J.W. Including my own mother. I take it back. This guy isn't just good. He's dangerous. The sooner Will tells everyone that he's the real J.W., the better.

The impostor finishes reading, and the room once again goes wild with applause. This is Brittany's cue to walk back to the podium. "Wasn't that just *brilliant*?" she gushes, causing the applause to start up again.

This time, I'm able to catch Will's gaze. I've never seen him look so furious. To everyone else he probably seems pensive, but the cold glint in his blue eyes sends a shiver down my spine. Not that I blame him for being angry.

"Ms. Anita Tremble, Mr. Quicksilver's personal assistant, will go around the room with a mic, so if you have any questions, please raise your hand," Brittany instructs.

I wait for Will for say something, but he doesn't. Instead we spend the next hour listening to this guy field questions about everything from his writing process to how he got his first "break" into publishing.

Why is Will letting this go on?

Maybe he's waiting for this guy to sink himself, only he doesn't. It's amazing how he manages to answer each question with just enough details to sound credible. How long has he been rehearsing this? I take it back again. This fake J.W. isn't just dangerous; he's a sociopath.

"We have time for one more question," says Brittany as she scans the upraised hands in the audience. "Oh! Let's hear from our very own head librarian." She points him out to Anita, who hands the mic over to Will.

Finally. I thought this would come sooner in the evening, but leave it to Will to wait until the last minute for maximum drama. I can hear him now. In a scene straight from Spartacus, he'll calmly pronounce, "I'm J.W. Quicksilver!" I can't wait to hear Mr. Highlander try to wiggle his way out of that one.

We wait for Will to say something, but he's silent.

The audience turns around to look at him. Will is staring at "J.W." with the same cold blue gaze as before. I'm starting to get twitchy. *Do it*! I scream inside. *Tell everyone that you're the real J.W. Quicksilver*!

The audience begins to shuffle nervously in their seats. Everyone is getting the impression that something isn't right.

"Well, man," drawls the fake J.W. "Spit it out. I canna answer a question unless you ask one."

Laughter sweeps through the room, causing Will's face to go red. "No question," he says tightly. "I just want to thank you for taking time from your busy schedule to come here tonight."

"It's been my pleasure," says the fake J.W., oblivious that he's addressing the very man he's impersonating.

Will hands the mic back to Anita.

Wait. *That's it*?

Brittany adds her thanks and instructs everyone who wants to purchase J.W.'s latest book to form a line to the right. I want to shout at the top of my lungs that they aren't getting an authentic J.W. Quicksilver autograph, but of course, I can't do that.

"Aren't you getting in line, Lucy?" asks Travis, shaking me out of my stupor.

"Maybe. When it dies down a little." I want to talk to this guy and see if I can figure out what his deal is, but more importantly, I need to talk to Will. "These heels are killing me. I'm not sure I'm up to standing in them for the next hour." Which isn't exactly a lie.

"I can hold your place in line for you," he offers.

"Really? You'd do that for me?"

"Sure. I have to admit, after listening to the guy, I'm intrigued. I might just have to buy a book for myself."

This is getting worse by the second. Betty Jean, sure. Shirley and the rest of the audience, understandable. But if someone as sharp as Travis can be taken in by this con man, then this town is in trouble.

I glance around the room at the few scattered persons who aren't in line and spy Will over by the bar. "Thanks. I'm going to take you up on your offer while I get a refill on my drink."

I head over to the bar, where Will is staring down into his glass like he's just lost his best friend. Which might very well happen if he doesn't man up soon. I liked angry Will better than this dejected version.

"What happened?" I hiss. "I thought you were going to tell everyone who you were."

"Not here, Lucy."

Not here? *Then where*? *And when*? I want to scream.

I glance over to see a familiar-looking door. If the layout of this place hasn't changed since my high school days, I'm pretty sure it leads to a storage room. Before he can protest, I grab Will by the elbow and drag him into the room, shutting the door firmly behind us.

Chapter Five

I FLIP ON THE lights. Good. The storage room is just I as remembered. No one will bother us in here.

"What are you doing?" Will asks, wild-eyed.

"What am I doing? What are *you* doing? What happened to telling everyone the truth?" I point to the door. "There's a con man out there impersonating you, and now he's taking money for a book he didn't write and signing your pen name to them. Don't you care?"

Will shoves a hand through his hair. "He must have bought those books off Amazon or ordered a bunch of copies from some other online site." He looks me in the eye. "He isn't making money off them. He would have to pay retail for those copies. And even if he didn't, he could make what? Maybe a few hundred dollars selling them? It makes no sense."

I'm a little less angry now, so I concentrate on what he just said. He's right. This doesn't make sense. "So, what's his angle?"

"I have no idea," he says grimly. "Other than to get his jollies pretending he's me."

"You have to admit, being you is pretty awesome. Did you see all those people out there? They're here because of you, Will. Because of the books you write. You should be the one out there reading your book out loud and getting applause. Not that ... Dougal MacKenzie wannabe."

He snickers at my *Outlander* reference. "Can you believe that phony accent?"

"You think it's phony?"

"It's about as real as the Loch Ness monster. The thing is, what's he up to? He has to know he'll get caught."

"How? Unless the real J.W. Quicksilver comes forward. Did you see how sneaky he was? Requesting that no one take pictures?"

"That doesn't guarantee anything. What's to stop someone from taking a picture and posting it online? Or telling the world on Facebook that they've met J.W. Quicksilver in the flesh?"

Will has a point. In this day of social media, there's no way this guy is going to get away with this scam. "I need to talk to him. Maybe I can ferret out what he's up to."

"You'll do that?"

"Yes, but you have to promise to tell Betty Jean the truth. You need to go to her book club meeting tomorrow night as yourself and schmooze up to everyone. Sign books. Answer questions. Pet Betty's Jean's cat. It's the only way you can make up for tonight's fiasco."

He tries to hide his smile. "Betty Jean has a cat?"

"I have no idea. But if she does, you'll do it. And anything else she asks. Within reason," I add quickly, because let's face it, this is Betty Jean we're talking about.

"Okay. You're right. I'll go to Betty Jean's and tell everyone I'm the real J.W. Quicksilver."

I heave a sigh of relief. "Thank God you've come to your senses." Will still looks miserable, so on impulse, I reach out and hug him.

The door to the storage room flies open, and we jump apart like a couple of guilty teenagers.

Travis stands in the doorway. "What's going on? I looked over and saw you pull Cunningham into the closet."

"I ... it's a storage room, not a closet," I clarify. "We were discussing, um, what kind of muffins I should bring to the book club meeting tomorrow night."

Ack. This is so lame.

I glance between both men. Travis and Will are staring each other down like they're ready to reenact the gunfight at the O.K. Corral. *Over me*?

I brush past Travis. "What's the line situation?"

"It's moving along," he says, still scowling. "I was standing behind a guy in a tweed suit and glasses. He's holding your place."

"You're not coming with me?"

"I'll join you in a minute. I want to have a word with Cunningham first."

Will grunts in agreement.

Oh, boy. The last thing I want is to leave these two alone, but I have no choice. Travis is right. The line is moving at a nice pace, and I can't miss this opportunity to have a talk with the fake J.W.

I weave my way back into the line, which is mostly composed of familiar faces, but there are more than a few people I've never seen before. Tourists, probably. It's not hard to find the gentleman Travis described. He's maybe in his mid-sixties, bald, and gives off a strong ex-professor vibe.

"Excuse me," I say. "My friend says you were saving my place in line?"

He nods pleasantly. "You must be Lucy. He didn't want you to lose your spot."

"Great reading, huh?"

"It was delightful," he says.

I try to hide my smile. Delightful isn't exactly how I'd describe *Assassin's Revenge*. "Big fan?"

"Oh, yes. I've read all the books in the series. How about you?"

"Only the last two, but I plan on catching up." I extend my hand. "Lucy McGuffin."

"Hoyt Daniels," he says, shaking my hand. "Nice to meet you."

A breeze swirls through the air, catching the little hairs on the back of my neck. That's odd, considering that we're indoors.

"You don't live in Whispering Bay, do you? I grew up here, and I'm pretty sure I know everyone in town. Unless ... you're a doughnut person?"

"Doughnuts?" He shudders. "No, I've never cared for them. All that sugar and I don't get along. And you're right. I don't live here in town. I was passing through, and I heard about this wonderful opportunity. I simply couldn't pass it up."

"You're lucky you got a ticket. I hear they sold out in the first hour."

"Right place at the right time. I thought I'd stay for a couple of days and enjoy the local hospitality."

"Then you should come to my café. The Bistro by the Beach. We make the best muffins in town. If you're concerned about your sugar intake, no worries. I always have one low-fat, low-sugar muffin on the menu. As a matter of fact, I'm working on a vegan low-fat chocolate zucchini muffin right now. I'm on my third round, and each time they get better." I dig into my purse and hand him a card. "First muffin is on the house."

He looks at the card, then places it inside his suit pocket. "Thank you, Lucy. I'll have to check it out."

The line moves up a few people, and we move along with it. A woman's high-pitched laugh draws my attention. Shirley is getting her book signed, and whatever this fake J.W. is saying to her has her giggling like a schoolgirl. "It appears our author has quite a way with women."

Hoyt follows my gaze. "It appears you're right." He frowns for a second, then his face smooths into a smile. "Tell me more about these muffins of yours. Do you have a favorite?"

"Not really. It depends on my mood. The apple walnut cream cheese is my signature muffin, but the mango coconut is pretty popular too. And there's the usual—lemon poppy seed, oat bran, chocolate chip, and of course, blueberry." I mention the blueberry because most people expect it, but it's my least favorite muffin to bake. It's not that I dislike it. It's just boring.

Shirley walks back with a book clutched to her chest. "Oh, Lucy! He's just so fabulous!" She opens the book. "Look what he wrote!"

I bend down to read the inscription. In bold lettering, it says: **To Shirley with the beautiful gray eyes. I enjoyed meeting you, lovely lady. Thank you for being such a loyal fan, J.W. Quicksilver**.

"He thinks I have beautiful eyes!" She runs around showing the inscription to anyone who'll look. A wave of anger nearly knocks me over. This guy isn't just hurting Will. He's hurting everyone who came out to see him today. He's playing with people's emotions, and he needs to be exposed as the worst kind of charlatan.

We inch our way closer to the man himself. The assistant, Anita, looks frazzled, directing traffic and taking credit cards and making change. I wonder if she's in on it as well. She has to be. There's no way she can be innocent. Brittany is helping with the transactions too, although it's more show, because she looks as cool as a cucumber.

"Looks like we're almost to the front of the line," says Hoyt.

I count six people ahead of us. "Yep." I glance back toward the bar area, where Will and Travis appear deep in conversation. What on earth could they be talking about? "So," I say to Hoyt in an attempt to take my mind off that, "which is your favorite of J.W.'s books?"

He ponders it a moment. "I'd have to say Assassin's Way, although they're all very good." He clears his throat. "You know, I don't usually tell this to strangers, but I'm an author as well."

The hair on my neck starts dancing a hula. It's official. Hoyt, or whatever his name is, is a big fat liar. "What do you write?"

"Thrillers. Very similar to the Assassin series, only my heroes are Navy Seals."

"Were you in the navy?"

"No, but I've done a lot of research."

"Oh, yeah? What's the title of one of your books?" I pull my cell phone from my purse and swipe to open up my Amazon account. Let's see how you answer this one, buddy.

"I'm not actually published. Yet." He pauses, then lowers his voice. "If I tell you something, can you keep it a secret?"

"Considering I've just met you and I don't know anyone who knows you, that probably won't be hard."

He flushes. "I must sound like a schoolboy. It's just I'm very excited. Mr. Quicksilver read my novel, and he's going to edit it."

I struggle to keep my expression neutral. "Oh, he is, is he?"

"He told me I had a lot of talent. And with some hard work I could become a published author."

"With a New York publisher?"

"Mr. Quicksilver is opening his own company. He's going to publish a select group of talented writers and help them get their big break. Not that I would call myself talented, but since ... "

"Mr. Quicksilver has?" I prompt.

He nods enthusiastically. "He's going to publish my book," he says proudly.

"Congratulations," I manage to choke out.

I think I have a pretty good idea where this is going, but I'm going to have to dig deeper to make certain. I just hope my acting skills are good enough to pull this off. I wet my lips and try to act nervous. "Hoyt, do you know if Mr. Quicksilver is looking for any more authors? For this publishing program of his?"

"Why? Do you know anyone who might be interested?"

"Actually... I do a little writing myself. Nothing up to Mr. Quicksilver's standards, or yours, I'm sure, but I've written a few romances."

He smiles indulgently. "I'd love to read one sometime."

The bigger the lie or the deception, the stronger my physical reaction. If I keep talking to this guy, I'm going to need a neck brace.

"So how much does he pay? For a novel?"

"You mean, as an advance?" He chuckles. "Oh no, Lucy, that's not how it's done. You see, publishing a novel is quite expensive. There's the copy editing, the formatting, the cover artist, and that's just the beginning. There's also a lot of promotion needed. Mr. Quicksilver is doing the developmental edits himself. He can't be expected to do that and pay for the rest of the expenses."

"So ... you paid him?"

"No need to look so worried, my dear. I've seen the charts. I should make my money back and double it within the first week alone. You could do the same yourself. If Mr. Quicksilver liked your work."

Something tells me that "Mr. Quicksilver" will most undoubtedly like my work. Or anyone else's, if they cough up the dough for this con of his.

I've never understood the expression seeing red before, but right now I'm seeing purple and every other color under the rainbow. He's running a publishing scam! And this guy is his accomplice. How many poor, unsuspecting saps have they taken in already?

"So, Hoyt, what do I have to do to get started? And is it very expensive?"

"He has a very easy payment plan. You could put down as little as five thousand dollars. You own your own business, so that shouldn't be a problem, right?"

"Five thousand?" I make a face. "I don't know—"

"Three thousand then. Don't waste this opportunity, Lucy. J.W. Quicksilver is going to personally edit and promote your novel. I can't think of money better spent."

"Let me think about it," I say.

"Don't think too long. There's just a few coveted spots left." He hands me a card with his number. "If you know any other aspiring authors who would be interested in the program and they sign up, Mr. Quicksilver might be able to waive your fee."

"Sounds like a great scheme."

"Doesn't it?" Hoyt says, not picking up on my sarcasm.

We get to the front of the line. Hoyt steps to the side and makes a flourishing motion with his arm, waving me on. "Ladies first."

"Thanks, don't mind if I do." I walk over to the table where Mr. Fakey Pants sits, surrounded by a stack of books that he didn't write but is taking credit for. He thinks he's King of the World. I'd love nothing more than to pick up one of those hardcover books and smash it over his head. I should probably mention this violent streak of mine during my next confession.

"Hello, my dear." The fake J.W. smiles up at me. "Can I sign a book for you?"

"Oh, yes, please."

He opens the book to the title page. "Who should I sign this to?"

I can't help but play with him a little. "How about to Lucy, your number one fan?"

He chuckles. "Ah. Excellent taste. I'm a Stephen King fan too," he says, referencing my quote from *Misery*.

"The man who wrote these books," I say, pointing to the stack in front of him, "I feel as if I've known that man all my life."

He pauses in the middle of signing. "Do you now, lassie?" He looks up at me with narrowed eyes, like he isn't sure what to make of our exchange.

I can't wait to see this guy and "Hoyt" taken away in handcuffs. I have to tell Travis what they're up to. No way is this their first rodeo. This little act of theirs is too polished. The problem is, how do I prove to Travis that this guy isn't the real J.W. Quicksilver without giving Will away? I could wait until Will's big announcement tomorrow at Betty Jean's book club, but by then it might be too late. They could skip town in the middle of the night.

My brain is scrambling with ideas when I realize I'm still holding on to my cell phone. My heart trips over in excitement. If I could just manage to take a photo of this guy …

Using my purse as a shield from detection, I hold my phone at waist level and aim it in his direction. "So, Mr. Quicksilver, what part of Scotland are you from?"

"Are you familiar with my homeland?" he asks, neatly evading my question.

Since I can't look through the camera lens, I'm not sure if I'm getting a good angle or not, so I snap as many pictures as possible. "Not really. But I'm a big *Outlander* fan. You've read the books, right? By Diana Gabaldon?"

"Read them? My dear, Diana and I are good friends. She actually comes to me for writing advice."

"Really?" I lean in closer to the table, allowing me to snap off a few more pictures, then blindly hit a couple of buttons on my phone.

I really hope this works. "You know, Mr. Quicksilver, I've written a romance, but I'm having a hard time getting it published." I glance back at Hoyt and smile. He gives me a thumbs-up.

"A romance?" The corner of J.W.'s mouth quirks up slightly. His condescending attitude ratchets up my anger a few more notches.

"My mother has read it, and she absolutely loves it. So do the rest of the ladies in her bridge club."

"I'd love to hear more about it. Perhaps we can find a time to meet while I'm here in town?"

"Gosh, that would be fabulous. I've already spoken to Hoyt about … you know, your special program."

"Have you?" He gives me an oily smile. "And you're interested?"

"Definitely. I have to work during the day, but I'll be at Betty Jean's book club meeting tomorrow night. I could bring you a copy of my manuscript."

"Perfect," he says. "I'll have my assistant make a note of it."

Before I can continue the conversation, Brittany waves me off to the side. "Lucy, you can't hog all of J.W.'s time," she scolds. "Are you paying with cash or credit card?"

I try to discreetly slide my phone back into the side pocket of my purse, but before I can manage it, Brittany blurts out, "You haven't been taking pictures, have you?"

I freeze. "What? No! Of course not."

Brittany and I lock gazes. She immediately makes an *oops, sorry* face. But it's too late. Anita, the assistant, has caught on. She puts out the palm of her hand. "Hand over your phone."

"Why? I haven't done anything wrong."

"Then you won't mind if I scroll through your picture gallery, do you?" she snaps back. Huh. Anita seemed a lot mousier five minutes ago.

I glance around the room. Everyone within hearing distance is star-ing at me.

Anita turns to Brittany. "Do you know this person? Do we need to call security?"

"No, of course not. Lucy," Brittany pleads, "hand over your phone."

I look over at the bar area, but I don't see Will. Has he left already? Travis is talking to my parents, oblivious to the fact that his date (not that I'm calling myself his date, but I'm pretty sure both he and my mother would) is about to be kicked out of the building.

I could walk away with my pictures. After all, what is Anita going to do? Have me arrested? Take away my phone? I'd like to see her try. This is a spanking brand-new iPhone 11. I stood in line two hours in the pouring rain outside the phone store the day it came out, used my free upgrade, and renewed my contract into the next century to get it at a decent price. But if I don't cow down to her, then Hoyt and the fake J.W. will know they can be exposed, and they might leave town before Travis can arrest them.

Reluctantly, I hand Anita the Hun my phone. She scrolls through my picture gallery with a pinched expression. "We specifically asked that no photos be taken tonight." She holds my phone up to my face. "You took two photos of Mr. Quicksilver. Erase them now."

There are over a dozen pictures of the signing table all taken from various angles, most of them fuzzy looking, one not so good photo of "Mr. Quicksilver" and one clear photo of him, which is impressive considering that I took these basically blindfolded. It kills me to erase them, but I have no choice. Anita inspects my phone to make sure I've deleted all the photos.

I try to sound beaten down. "I'm sorry. I didn't mean to break the rules, but I was just so overwhelmed with excitement." I turn to "J.W." and make a cringy face. "I hope this doesn't ruin our arrangement?"

Like a rock star who's used to his fans getting out of line, he smiles indulgently. "No worries, my dear. I completely understand."

I take my "autographed" book and head toward the door, where Travis is waiting for me. "Where's Will?" I ask. "And what were you two talking about for so long?"

"Nothing," Travis says vaguely. "And I have no idea where he is. He probably went to the bathroom or something." He points to the book in my hand. "So, how was meeting the great J.W. Quicksilver in person?"

"Horrible."

The valet brings us Travis's car. Once we're alone, he turns in his seat to face me. "What do you mean, horrible?" His expression tightens. "Did Quicksilver make a pass at you?"

"Never mind that. Did you get my text?"

"What text?"

"Just check your phone before I explode."

Travis pulls his cell phone from his jacket pocket and swipes his screen open. He studies it intently. "Is this supposed to turn me on? Because if it is, it's working."

What? I grab the phone from his hand. Oh no. It's the selfie I took of myself in the miniskirt to play with Brittany's head.

"I didn't mean to send you that. It was supposed to be a joke on Brittany." I scroll through the other pictures in the text. To my relief, they're all there, including the fuzzy ones and ... Yes! Staring back at me is a clear as day photo of the man signing books this evening.

"Let me explain," I say. "I took a bunch of pictures tonight—"

"Even though we were explicitly told not to?"

"So I broke the rules. Sue me. I took a bunch of pictures, but I was afraid I might get caught, which I did, thanks to Brittany's big mouth, but I was able to blind-text them to you before they made me delete them." I hold the screen up to show him the photo. "This is what I texted you."

Travis looks amused. "I don't know. This one isn't doing anything for me. I liked the other picture better."

"Ha ha. Pay attention. I texted you this picture because ... this man? The one who charmed everyone with his reading tonight and autographed books? This man is *not* J.W. Quicksilver."

Chapter Six

TRAVIS'S GRIN FADES. "WHAT do you mean? If this isn't J.W. Quick-silver, then who is he?"

"That's what I need you to find out. Can you run this picture through a facial recognition program?"

"I work for the Whispering Bay Police Department. This isn't Quantico." Travis starts the engine. "Let's save this for somewhere more private."

Good idea. We drive back to The Bistro and head into the kitchen. The first thing I do is let Paco out to do his business, then kick off my heels and put on a pot of coffee. We're going to need caffeine to get through this conversation. On a whim, I reach up into a cabinet and retrieve a tin full of yesterday's muffins. "Want one?" I offer.

He opts for a cinnamon streusel. When Travis first moved to town, he told me he was a "doughnut" man, but he quickly wised up and switched his allegiance to team muffin.

My cell phone pings. I pull it out of my purse. It's Will. **I'll call you later**, I text.

Travis glances curiously at my phone, but he doesn't ask. He leans against the counter and takes a sip of his coffee. "What makes you think the man we saw tonight wasn't J.W. Quicksilver?"

"For one thing, he's lying. He's not Scottish, and he didn't write those books."

"Because the hair on the back of your neck told you?"

"Basically, yes."

He sighs. "Lucy, we've been through this before. I admit, you've got great instincts, but there's no way you can always tell if someone is lying or telling the truth. Statistically, it's impossible."

"Is everything always so black and white with you? Don't you think that *maybe* there could be an alternative explanation for some things?"

"Not in my line of work. You're either guilty or you're not." He breaks off a piece of his muffin and offers it to Paco, who gobbles it down. "Here's one thing we can agree on. You were right about this little guy. He wasn't trained as a cadaver dog."

"What finally brought you to your senses?"

"I've researched pretty much every program out there, and none of them has ever used this kind of dog before."

"So how do you account for Paco's ability to—*wait*." A tiny spider of fear crawls up my spine. "You really did investigate this?"

"I told you I was going to look into it."

Before Paco came to live with me, he was owned by Susan Van Dyke, whose murder I solved. But his history before Susan is unknown. According to Susan's staff, she found the dog wandering down the street without a collar and unchipped. Who was his original owner? What if he or she shows up on my doorstep one day wanting Paco back? I could never give him up. Not after everything we've been through together.

"Stop investigating," I say firmly.

"No worries. I've already figured out how Paco finds"—he makes air quotes with his fingers—"the dead bodies."

"Oh, yeah?" This should be interesting. "How?"

"Since Paco is with you most of the time, it only makes sense that he'd come across the dead bodies because you're the one who's finding them. And you're finding them because you just so happen to be in the right place at the right time." He then proceeds to go through, one by one, all the bodies I've found, starting with Abby Delgado, the victim from my first murder investigation, and "logically" explains it all. I wonder how long it took him to come up with all this.

I give up.

I'm never going to convince Travis that I'm a human lie detector or that Paco sees ghosts, so I'm not going to try anymore. Which answers the question I've been struggling with these past couple of weeks. Any chance that Travis and I could end up together is gone. There's absolutely no way I can be with someone who doesn't believe me when I tell them the most essential thing about myself.

It all makes sense. I've always believed that Will is my soul mate. I've been in love with him forever. He's my best friend. When I was seven, he saved me from a squirrel attack, which is no small thing. And most importantly, he's always believed in me. Maybe not completely, since he never told me he was J.W. Quicksilver, but he's never questioned my abilities.

"What's wrong?" asks Travis. "You look like you just found out there was a national ban on muffins."

"What?" I shake myself back into the conversation. "Nothing's wrong. Except that the man we saw tonight is not J.W. Quicksilver."

"Not that again. Exactly how do you know this?" he challenges.

This is where things get dicey, because I can't prove it without telling him about Will, so I try another tack. I tell him all about Hoyt Daniels and the publishing scam he and the fake J.W. are running.

Travis considers this a few moments. "That does sound shady, but it doesn't prove that he isn't J.W. Quicksilver."

"Think about it. Why would a famous author like J.W. Quicksilver need to take people's money? It makes no sense."

He pulls out his phone and studies the picture of the fake J.W., then starts typing in a few notes. "And the guy in the line who tried to get you to buy into this scheme said his name was Hoyt Daniels?" I nod. "Okay. I'll run that name through a few programs and see what I can come up with."

"Really?"

"Sure. But only because, like you said, the whole thing sounds like a con. That is the kind of evidence I can work with, Lucy."

Right. As opposed to the "woo-woo" stuff.

"Are you still going to Betty Jean's book club meeting tomorrow night?" he asks.

"Oh, you better believe it."

"Why are you smiling? And why am I suddenly nervous as hell?"

I'm smiling because tomorrow night, not only is this faker going to be exposed, Will is going to tell everyone that he's the real J.W. Quicksilver. I can't wait to see the look on everyone's faces when they find out, especially Betty Jean's. Not that I plan to gloat or anything. But, yeah, I plan to gloat. Heavily, as a matter of fact.

"No reason to be nervous," I say.

"Now I'm terrified. Promise me you're going to let me handle this."

"I promise." And I mean it too. Now that I've alerted the police about the con and Will has promised to tell everyone the truth, I can rest easy. "Sorry to kick you out, but I need to go to bed. Tomorrow's going to get here before you know it, and I have muffins to bake."

Travis nods toward my kitchen door. "Don't forget to—"

"Lock up," I finish for him.

But instead of leaving like I thought he would, we stand there, staring at one another. The room feels overly warm. Did I leave the oven on by mistake? Travis leans in close, like he's about to kiss me.

His mouth is just a few inches away when I blurt, "You need to delete that photo of me."

He stops cold. "The one you sent me tonight?"

"The one I *accidentally* sent you tonight."

"Why would I delete it?"

"Because it's awful. And ... What if it ends up on the Internet? Or in some chat group?"

He looks like he's about to laugh but wisely refrains. "First off, it's not awful. It's sexy ... in a cute way. Secondly, I don't plan to share it with anyone."

"Then what's the big deal about deleting it?"

"Lucy," he says, his lips hovering dangerously close to mine. "Don't you trust me?"

Oh boy. Yep. He's going to kiss me. Only I can't let that happen on account of I'm in love with Will. Before he can make a move, I shove him out the door, slamming it firmly behind him. "Drive safe!"

He chuckles from the other side. "Good night, Lucy."

I lean against the wooden door, listening to the sound of his footsteps crunching against the gravel parking lot. Despite all his irritating qualities, Travis is a good guy. And yeah, not so hard to look at either. He's going to make some girl deliriously happy. It's just not going to be me.

The thought of Travis and some anonymous "other girl" makes me frown. Then I mentally shake my head. I can't have my cake and eat it too. I'll be in a relationship with Will, which is what I've always wanted. I should be doing cartwheels. Correction: I will be doing cartwheels. Just as soon as this whole J.W. Quicksilver mess is over with.

I call Will to tell him about the fake publishing scam.

"That bastard," Will seethes. "So that's what he's up to."

"Yeah. Good thing Travis is on the case."

"You told Fontaine?"

I'm not sure why Will's attitude bothers me, but it does. If he had just told everyone the truth tonight, Hoyt Daniels and the fake J.W. would already be behind bars.

"I didn't tell him that you were J.W. Quicksilver, if that's what you mean. But yeah, I told him all about the scam. I even got a picture of the guy impersonating you on my cell phone. Travis is going to see if he can find out who this joker really is."

"Good idea," he says grudgingly.

"So, I've been ordered to be at Betty Jean's house by six. What time are you going to get there?"

"Why? What does it matter?"

"Because this is what I think you should do. Book club starts at seven. You should show up around twenty minutes later, that way we'll make sure to have a full house. And just when everyone is lapping up all the BS this faker is spilling, you stand up and announce that you're the real J.W. Want me to tape it with my new cell phone?"

"Tape it?" he croaks.

"Sure! Think about it. It could be awesome publicity for your books. Not that you need publicity, but it could definitely be useful in court."

"I don't know, Lucy. Isn't it enough that I'm going to expose the guy? Do we have to have it on tape?"

Yes. But I suppose after all this time hiding his real identity, it's hard for Will to fathom going so public.

"Okay, no tape," I concede, "but I definitely think we need a police presence. What if this guy gets violent? Or tries to escape? I'll let Travis know that he needs to be at the book club meeting. He might already have the guy's ID by then. I bet he's wanted all over the place for a bunch of different scams."

Will doesn't say anything. I wonder if this is a good time to tell him that yes, we're together now. Nah. That's something we should talk about in person.

We say our goodbyes, then Paco and I head up the stairs to bed. I wiggle my way out of the black dress and carefully hang it back up in my closet when my cell phone pings. Probably Will with something he forgot to tell me about tomorrow night.

Only when I swipe open my screen, it's not Will. It's Travis. But instead of a text, he's sent a photo of himself wearing a woman's dress, high heels, and a red wig. He looks ... awful.

I burst out laughing. **What**?? I text, then add a smiley face for good measure.

His response: **This was taken at a Halloween party a few years back**.

I want to know more about this Halloween party where Travis dressed in drag. And I should definitely let him know that tonight was our first and last "date." But that also seems like more of a face-to-face conversation.

I love it, I text back.

Good, cause now we're even. You don't show anyone mine and I won't show anyone yours.

I can't help but go to bed with a smile on my face.

Chapter Seven

I WAKE UP AT 3 a.m., too wound up to go back to sleep. Not only do I need to bake fresh muffins for The Bistro's regular breakfast crowd, I have to come up with a special batch for the big book club meeting. And these can't be just any old muffins. They must be spectacular because the events of tonight will be talked about for years to come. Tonight, Whispering Bay will find out that the real J.W. Quicksilver has been living among us all this time, and a con man will be hauled off to jail.

I can see everyone now, giddy with excitement over the news, getting the *real* J.W. to sign their books, sipping wine, and munching on my muffins, which will be forever linked to one of the greatest nights in Whispering Bay history. Ha! Take that, Heidi.

I spend the next couple of hours baking myself into a tizzy. At exactly five, Jill, who works for us, arrives and starts prepping for breakfast. Sarah comes flying through the back door fifteen minutes later. "Sorry! I overslept." Which is unusual, because Sarah never oversleeps, as opposed to myself, who's been known to hit my snooze button more than a couple of times.

"No big deal," I say. "Everything's good to go."

Her gaze sweeps over the mountain of baked goods on the kitchen counter. "Looks like someone didn't get much sleep last night." She gives me a sly look. "So how was your date with Travis? Did you pull off the dress? Never mind, of course you pulled it off."

"It wasn't a date. And ... I think I looked okay."

"I'm sure you looked way better than okay," says Sarah.

Jill picks up a muffin and studies it. "Is this a new flavor?"

"Kind of. I was waiting to unveil it next month, but I couldn't wait. It's a raspberry white chocolate muffin."

Jill takes a bite and makes an I-just-died-and-went-to-heaven face. "Oh, Lucy, this is fabulous."

This is exactly the reaction I'm looking for. "Thanks. They're for Betty Jean's book club tonight."

Jill finishes off the muffin in three bites. "So, what was J.W. Quick-silver like?"

"He's something else." I wish I could tell them the truth, but they'll find out soon enough.

We finish prepping, and the café opens at exactly six. Paco takes his place by my feet as I stand behind the counter and take orders. The first couple of hours go by quickly. The early morning crowd is mostly people on their way to work. Once it hits eight, we cater to an older crowd sprinkled with younger stay-at-home mom and dad types or people who work from home but need to get away from their desk. Since we provide excellent coffee, free Wi-Fi, and a killer view of the gulf, I don't blame them.

Viola Pantini and Gus Pappas, Whispering Bay's cutest over-sixty couple, walk through the door. "Lucy," says Viola, "I didn't get a chance to speak to you last night, but I wanted to tell you how wonderful you looked."

"What a night, huh?" says Gus. "I can't believe we're lucky enough to see J.W. Quicksilver two nights in a row."

"It's one of the perks of being in Betty Jean's book club," Viola muses. "You'll be there tonight, right?"

"Believe me, I wouldn't miss it for the world. I'll be introducing a new muffin. Raspberry white chocolate."

"Sounds yummy," says Viola. They order their breakfast, and I hand them their coffees.

My parents are the next in line, followed by more of the Gray Flamingos. No one can stop talking about last night and how awesome this fake J.W. was. *Bleh*. It's killing me to keep Will's secret. I glance at my watch. Not too much longer now.

I'm standing behind the counter minding my own business when the unthinkable happens. Heidi Burrows walks into my café. She's been here before but never without a good reason. Even though I just checked the time, I check it again. What on earth is Heidi doing in The Bistro in the middle of a workday? Shouldn't she be at her bakery selling overpriced doughnuts laden with cholesterol to unsuspecting potential heart attack victims?

"Good morning, Lucy." Heidi is just a few years older than me and, like her famous literary namesake, blonde. She inherited the bakery from her mother, who inherited it from her mother. Don't get me wrong. I love the idea of a business that's been passed down through three generations, especially when that business is a bakery, but Heidi thinks that because her recipes are ancient that she's better than everyone else. Or at least, her doughnuts are.

"Hello, Heidi."

She glances around the café. "Business looks good."

"Why wouldn't it be?"

"I know the last time we talked I was a bit brusque, but you'll be happy to know that I've forgiven you."

"You've forgiven me?"

"Lucy," she says, deadpan, "you stood in this very room and practically accused me of murder."

Well, she has a point. "It was nothing personal. I was trying to catch a killer."

"And you succeeded. Eventually."

Leave it to Heidi to compliment me, then follow up with a dig. "I hear you're providing doughnuts for the diocesan lecture series. Jesus and Doughnuts? That's generous of you."

"We all have to do our part for the community. Don't you agree?"

"Of course. We're just one big, happy family, aren't we?"

"I like to think so. You'll be happy to know I've decided to take your advice about reducing the fat content in my doughnuts. Today's consumer wants healthier options. To run a successful business, you have to stay flexible so you can react to the marketplace."

I grit my teeth and smile. Now Heidi is lecturing me straight out of a marketing 101 course. As if I don't know how to run a business!

Sarah comes out from the kitchen looking uncharacteristically flustered. "I just realized you were here," she says to Heidi.

"I hope I'm not too early," Heidi says.

Sarah gives me a quick sideways look. "Just a little, but it's okay."

"Too early for what?" I ask, confused.

"You didn't tell her?" Heidi asks Sarah.

"Tell me what?"

"Heidi wanted to take a look around our kitchen," Sarah explains. "And I thought another time we'd go over and take a look at her kitchen. You know, to compare notes on efficiency, that kind of thing."

The hair on my neck tingles. I don't think I've ever caught Sarah in a lie before. And if I have, it's been something so benign it didn't matter, but this lie about Heidi feels like a slap in the face.

First Will, then Sebastian, and now Sarah.

This is one of those times when my gift feels like the worst curse in the world. If I was like everyone else, I'd be blissfully unaware that my good friend and business partner, a woman I admire, has just lied to me.

I swallow hard. "Oh. Sure. That makes sense."

Sarah smiles at me, but it's the same kind of smile that you'd give to your dog before you take him to the vet to get neutered. *Trust me, I'm only doing this for your own good*. She leads Heidi back to the kitchen area, leaving me with a brain full of disturbing images, most of them centering around Heidi either sabotaging my oven or stealing my recipe box. It's like we've let the fox inside the henhouse. What's Sarah thinking?

The door to The Bistro opens, and in walks Victor Marino. "Good morning, Lucy!" At the sound of Victor's voice, Paco slinks down, trying to make himself smaller. I really hope Victor isn't going to pester me this morning about involving Paco in a séance. I'm mentally preparing to turn him down again when Victor says, "Glorious day, isn't it? I don't think I've ever been so happy to be alive."

Okay. Something is definitely not right here. Victor is one of the more upbeat members of the Sunshine Ghost Society, but I don't think I've ever seen him so downright cheerful. But it's that last statement that feels off. *Happy to be alive?* Victor lives for the day he passes over to the other side and becomes one with the spirit world (his words, not mine).

I look out the window facing the gulf. "It's actually a bit overcast, but yeah, not too bad."

He chuckles. "I'm in such a good mood, I didn't even notice."

"Really? Been communing with the spirits?" I ask, fully expecting to be regaled with a story about his latest ghostly encounter.

"Not exactly." He glances around like he doesn't want to be overheard. "Can you keep a secret?"

Uh-oh. I've heard this before. "Sure."

"I'm not supposed to tell anyone yet, but I think I'll burst if I can't share my good news. I'm going to be published! I've secretly been working on my autobiography for the past two years. Oh, I know that face," he says at my expression. "Autobiographies can be so dull. Never fear. It's the story of my life, yes, but it's hidden in a very intricate fictionalized plot not unlike the ... *The Da Vinci Code*. Not that I would ever compare my writing to an author as famous as Dan Brown."

"Don't tell me J.W. Quicksilver is going to help you?"

"As a matter of fact, yes." He frowns. "How did you know?"

"Lucky guess." I wave him over to the edge of the counter, where we won't be overheard. "I'm sorry to be indiscreet, but did you give him money?" Victor retired from a forty-year career at the post office. I hate to think of even a dime of Victor's hard-earned pension in the hands of that smooth-talking fraud.

Victor's cheeks go red. "I really can't discuss the fine points of our contract."

"You signed a contract? Did you have an attorney look it over?"

"I wasn't born yesterday. Hoyt isn't just an attorney. He specializes in literary contracts."

"Hoyt? As in Hoyt Daniels?"

Victor looks pleased. "You've heard of him too? He was at the signing last night. Mr. Quicksilver is one of his clients. He only represents big authors."

"I've heard of him all right."

"Please don't tell anyone, Lucy. Hoyt says that these contracts can fall through for anything."

I nod, too angry to think about anything other than how many more Victors are out there this morning. I wonder if Travis has had any luck with the photo I sent him?

I take Victor's order, then head into the kitchen, where Jill is by herself, assembling a sandwich. "Where's Sarah? And Heidi?" I ask.

"They're in the pantry going over inventory."

Sarah is showing Heidi our inventory?

Something Sarah said to me yesterday reruns through my brain. When Sarah offered me the money I borrowed from Will, she said she had a few ideas about how I could pay her back, only I didn't get a chance to ask her what she meant by that.

"Everything okay?" Jill asks.

I shake away the bad juju from my brain. I'll deal with this after tonight.

"Sure. Everything's peachy. Do you mind if I cut out early? We close in twenty minutes, and there's no one at the counter. I need to see Travis."

Jill smirks. "Yesterday it was Will, and today it's Travis. You sure do have an interesting life."

"You don't know the half of it," I mutter.

Chapter Eight

CINDY, THE RECEPTIONIST FOR the Whispering Bay Police Department, is on a perpetual quest to lose the universally elusive last five pounds, but she has a weakness for my cranberry muffins, and I'm more than happy to cater to it. "These are low-fat." I set a bag of muffins on her desk.

Her eyes go rounder than a blueberry. "Thanks!" She opens a drawer and pulls out a dog bone. "I got these just in case you ever brought Paco back for a visit." She holds the bone in the air above Paco's head. "Sit," she instructs.

Paco turns to look at me as if to say, *I got this*. He sits.

"Good boy," says Cindy. "Down."

Paco goes into the down position like he's been doing it all his life. "Now stay," she commands.

After he "stays" for a full ten seconds, she gives him the treat. "You've done such a good job with him, Lucy. He's so well trained."

I wish I could take credit for this "training," but I had no idea that Paco knew the down and stay command because I've never asked him to do it. Maybe this is something he learned from a previous owner. Or maybe ... He munches on the bone with a self-satisfied look on his face. Besides the ability to sniff out dead bodies, I swear this little guy can understand human language. I'd give anything to see inside that smarty-pants brain of his, even for just a few minutes.

"I've been thinking of getting a dog too," says Cindy. "So Rusty and I've been watching that show with the dog guy to get advice."

"Dog guy?"

"Yeah, you know, Woofio? He's a more modern, cool version of that Cesar guy."

"Never heard of him. What kind of name is Woofio?"

Cindy giggles. "Don't you get it? Woof-io? You should watch the show. He's absolutely brilliant at getting dogs to do things they don't want to do."

"I don't know. Paco is pretty perfect just the way he is." My dog looks up at me with a pleased expression. "So, Cindy, is Travis busy?"

"I heard you two went to the big event last night." She winks at me. "Congratulations on snagging him, by the way."

"What? Oh, no, Travis and I aren't—never mind. Is he in? I really need to speak to him."

She lowers her voice. "He's in, but he's on a really important call at the moment. Top secret. Very hush-hush. I probably shouldn't have said anything."

When I don't take the bait, she tells me anyway. "With the FBI," she mouths silently.

Travis is on the phone with the FBI? This must be about the photo! At this very moment, he could be finding out the fake J.W.'s real identity.

"Wow. What do you think that's about?" Even though I know exactly what that's about.

She shrugs. "Who knows? But this isn't his first call from that Agent Billings. She's probably called at least three times in the past couple of weeks that I'm aware of."

What?

At the look on my face, Cindy backtracks. "Not that there's anything going on between them."

A few weeks ago, the feds, under the direction of Agent Patricia Billings, ran an operation here in Whispering Bay to hide Joey "The Weasel" Frizzone from the mob. The goal was to keep Joey alive so he could testify against Chicago's biggest Don, Vito Scarlotti. For a while, dead bodies were popping up everywhere, and it looked like Joey was about to get his lights punched out until Paco and I uncovered a notorious mob assassin, "El Tigre," and defused the situation.

Maybe Agent Billings has been keeping Travis abreast of the case. Although the last I'd seen in the news, Joey testified, and Vito was found guilty.

Cindy looks down at the desk phone. "Oh! They're done talking. Want me to buzz you through the door?"

"If you don't mind, thanks."

Paco and I make our way through the station to the conference room, where I find Travis and Zeke Grant, Whispering Bay's chief of police, with their heads together like they're powwowing. Zeke spots me first. "Lucy," he says, "What can I do for you?"

"Sorry to interrupt, but I was wondering if I could speak to Travis?"

"Sure." Zeke turns to Travis. "I'm going home early this afternoon. You okay to handle things here at the station?"

"Not a problem, chief."

Zeke takes a minute to rub the top of Paco's head. "Hey, little guy. Seen any dead bodies lately?"

Travis shakes his head as if to say, *Don't encourage her*.

"You'll be the first person we call if he comes across one," I say pleasantly.

"Say hi to Mimi for me," I call to Zeke on his way out the door. Zeke's wife, Mimi, is the town's mayor. She gave birth to twins a couple of months ago. Two babies, a son in middle school, and a daughter in college. I have no idea how they do it.

"I can't imagine being mayor and the chief of police and taking care of one baby, let alone two," I say.

"They're busy, all right." Travis looks at his watch. "Speaking of busy, it's not yet two. What are you doing here? Did you close early?"

"Not exactly. I just saw Victor Marino. Guess who's going to help Victor publish a fictional version of his autobiography?"

Travis's expression tightens. "J.W. Quicksilver."

"I told you, he's not J.W. Quicksilver. By the way, I hear you were on the phone with the FBI."

"How do you know that?"

Rats. Me and my big mouth. I don't want to get Cindy in trouble. For one thing, I really like her, and if she finds out I told Travis what I wasn't supposed to tell anyone, she might start clamming up on me. "I, um, overheard you and Zeke down the hallway," I fudge.

He nods grudgingly, which tells me my wild stab was right on point.

"I was talking to Agent Billings," says Travis. "You remember her, right? I just sent her the photo. She's looking into it."

"What does Zeke think?"

"He thinks it sounds shady."

"Good. Because it is shady. I couldn't get Victor to tell me how much money he's already given to this con man, but you can get it back, right?"

"Let's not jump to any conclusions. If this guy is running a scam, we have to be able to prove it. Then the victims have to file a complaint. And then there's the question as to whether this guy is who says he is. There's a lot of ifs here, Lucy."

Not really. Which Travis will discover tonight. Just a few more hours to go ...

"So, how is Agent Billings?"

"Okay, I guess."

"Did you two catch up on the Vito Scarlotti case?"

"Not really. I was more interested in seeing what she could find out about this guy from last night."

"But she has called to update you on the case, right?"

"Lucy, the FBI has more important things to do than call some small-town cop and fill him in on their cases."

"So you haven't spoken to her since she left Whispering Bay?"

"Nope."

Oh boy. The hair on the back of my neck is doing a jig. *Travis has just lied to me.*

I try to conjure up a mental picture of Patricia Billings in my head. Late thirties, medium height, FBI field-standard fit body. With her light brown hair always pulled back in a bun and a no-nonsense look in her eyes, she's hardly femme fatale material, but there's a sharpness about her that most men would probably find interesting.

Could Travis and Patricia Billings be involved?

They must be. Otherwise, why lie to me about their phone calls? Sure, he and I aren't a "couple," but he's the one who's been trying to make that happen. Not me.

I try to swallow past the lump of disappointment clogging my throat. People lie to me every day about all sorts of silly things, but between this and Sarah lying about Heidi's reason for being in the café ... It's too much.

I pick Paco up off the floor and hug him. A woman's best friend is definitely her dog. "Do you think you can come to Betty Jean's book club meeting tonight?"

"Why would I do that?"

"So you can make an arrest."

"That's jumping the gun, don't you think?"

"Then consider it your civic duty to attend. Didn't Zeke just tell you to handle things? Because I can guarantee that tonight, something big is going to go down at the meeting."

Travis's eyes narrow. "Like what?"

"Like ... just promise me you'll come. Seven o'clock. Betty Jean Collins's house."

"I don't know where she lives," he says stubbornly.

"You're a cop. Look up her address."

Chapter Nine

I'm still reeling from Travis's lie about Agent Billings, but I need to focus on tonight. Hopefully, Will isn't flipping out. He promised me he'd be at Betty Jean's house and make everything right, and I trust he'll keep his word, but he has to be anxious. Has he let his publisher and agent know what he's going to do?

As his best friend and future girlfriend, I should lend him my moral support.

I stop by the library. Faith tells me that Will has left for the day, so I swing by his house, but there's no answer when I knock on the door. I call his cell, but it goes to voice mail. Huh. Maybe he went to go shoot some pool or get some last-minute advice from Sebastian. Since I have a few hours before I need to show up at Betty Jean's, I stop by the rectory.

"Hey, Lucy." Shirley is all decked out like she's going to the prom. Big hair. Big rhinestone earrings. Sparkly dress.

"You look fancy."

Shirley pats her hair. "I went to the salon this morning. Wasn't last night fabulous? And to think we get J.W. all to ourselves tonight! I don't think I've been this excited since the St. Petersburg Boys Choir came to sing for us last Easter." Shirley must be easy to please, because it was St. Petersburg, Florida, not Russia.

"Yeah, sure. Last night was great." I sound wooden, but pretending to be excited about this faker is getting old. I glance at my watch. Two hours to go until this charade is over. "Is my brother in?"

"Sorry, hon, he went to do some home visits."

"Do you know if Will came by to see him? Or called him maybe?"

"Not that I'm aware. But he could have come by while I was out getting my hair done." Shirley frowns. "Everything okay?"

"Sure, everything is fine," I lie.

She goes back to filing papers. "See you this evening at Betty Jean's," she says cheerfully.

Paco and I go back to the car, and I try Will's cell again, but nothing. Where can he be? And why isn't he answering his phone? I'm probably making a big deal out of nothing, but my Spidey sense tells me that something isn't right.

I try to shake off this feeling of dread. It's only natural that my woo-woo clock is ringing off its base right now. The past few days have been crazy. I can't wait to wake up tomorrow to normalcy. Normal for me, that is.

We head back to my apartment above The Bistro. I take a quick shower and put on the new T-shirt I threatened to wear to last night's book signing, I LIKE BIG MUFFINS AND I CANNOT LIE. If anything, it will be good for a laugh, which we might all need tonight.

I place the muffins in a protective container, then take Paco for a quick walk around the building before we head out. I'm early, but I thought I'd run by Will's house one more time on my way to Betty Jean's. I'm loading up my car when Brittany's red Mustang squeals into The Bistro parking lot. She jumps out of her car. "Thank God I've found you! Something disastrous has just happened."

Disastrous for Brittany can be anything from a broken nail to finding pickles in her tuna salad sandwich. What she needs is a good stiff dose of reality. "Calm down. What's wrong now?"

"You're never going to believe this." She scrunches up her face like she can't bear to tell me. "J.W. Quicksilver is a fake."

Finally. "Oh, I believe it all right. So Will told you the whole story?"

"Will? What's he got to do with this?" Brittany begins pacing around the parking lot in her high heels, and she never wobbles once, which is impressive. "I'm going to be the laughingstock of the ACCE!"

"The what?"

"The Association of Chamber of Commerce Executives. Lucy, do you think they'll kick me out? Or ... do you think I'll get"—her voice drops to a horrified whisper—"*fired*?"

"Brittany, I'm confused. Tell me what's going on."

Paco makes a movement with his head suspiciously close to a nod. It's like he's agreeing with me. *From the beginning, please.*

"Remember I was telling you about my plans to hold a book festival here in town? I contacted J.W.'s publisher to let him know how thrilled we were to have J.W. here and how we'd love to have him back for another event and to see if possibly we could get some other big-name authors here too."

"Like Lee Child?"

Brittany winces. "Don't remind me. I feel so ... " She shrugs it off, but I'm pretty sure the word "foolish" was on the tip of her tongue. "Anyway, I got an email back this afternoon from the publisher. He had no idea what I was talking about. He said J.W. doesn't do public events. At first, I thought maybe it was a standard reply, but the wording wasn't right, so I called."

"You talked to his publisher?"

"To an assistant. She told me that there was no way that J.W. Quicksilver did any kind of public appearance and that we were being bamboozled. My entire professional reputation is at stake here. I'm the one who insisted we do the big event at Daddy's restaurant last night. All those people who came and bought tickets … Do you think I could be arrested? For aiding and abetting in a scam?" She bends over and rests her hands on her knees like she's sucking for air.

"Take slow, deep breaths," I urge. Then, for good measure, I rub her back. The last thing I need is for Brittany to start hyperventilating and pass out in my parking lot.

"I don't know who this impostor is, but I even got the Chamber of Commerce to comp him a beach house while he was in town. I'm not a violent person, but I could absolutely kill him."

Yikes. "I'm sorry."

She straightens up to look me in the eye. Her gaze sharpens. "Why don't you seem surprised by any of this?"

I might as well tell Brittany everything. Or at least, the parts that are mine to tell. "Because I know who the real J.W. Quicksilver is."

For a few seconds, she's speechless. But Brittany being Brittany, she recovers quickly. "You do? But how? Where is he? Is he here in town?"

"I can't tell you. Not yet anyway."

"Who else knows about this?"

"Just me, the real J.W. Quicksilver, and Travis. Well, Travis doesn't know the identity of the real J.W., but I warned him that the man we saw last night was an impostor. *That's* why I was trying to get a picture of him. So Travis could run it through a facial recognition program."

Brittany looks duly chastised. "I didn't mean to rat you out. It just sort of popped out of my mouth. But oh, Lucy, you're so clever! Was Travis able to identify him?"

"Not yet, but this guy is running a publishing scam here in town. He's taken money from Victor Marino and who knows how many other people. And I'll bet you my last muffin tin that it's not the first scam he's pulled."

Brittany goes pale. "This is getting worse by the second." She looks around the parking lot and spots my car with the door open and the container of muffins sitting on the seat. "Are you still going to Betty Jean's book club tonight?"

"Yep. We have to pretend everything is status quo or we might scare this con man and his gang into skipping town. If that happens, we might never find out who he is or recoup the money he's stolen."

"Gang? You mean—"

"Anita the assistant and a man who's going by the name of Hoyt Daniels. Maybe there's more too. Who knows? Once they get to Betty Jean's, we have to act like everything's normal. Then the real J.W. Quicksilver is going to show up and tell everyone who he is. Travis will arrest the bad guys and, voila! Everything will be fixed." *Hopefully*.

"That's brilliant! Except ... I hope no one will blame me for any of this."

"Why should they blame you? You're just as much a victim here as anyone else."

"You're right." She squares back her shoulders. "In some ways, I'm probably his biggest victim. This is all Betty Jean's fault. She's the one who brought him to town. She should have done a better job of vetting him. First, he conned me into throwing him that huge party at Daddy's and then he conned the city out of a free beach house. I'll probably have to testify against him in court. Don't you think? I might even be the prosecution's star witness." She reaches out and grabs me in a hug. "I knew I was right to come to you with this! Thank you, Lucy! I feel *so* much better."

Now that this crisis is taken care of, Brittany can focus on more important things. She reads the slogan on my T-shirt and tsks. "At least you didn't wear that last night. You were playing with me, weren't you? When you sent me that horrible picture of you in the miniskirt?"

Travis didn't think it was so horrible.

"I hope you learned your lesson. No fashion advice. Unless I ask for it."

She makes an X over her chest. "Promise." Her eyes go sparkly. "But if I *was* to give you some fashion advice, I would tell you to wear exactly what you wore last night, down to the last little detail. You looked wonderful! Travis couldn't take his eyes off you."

I get all twitchy. "That's probably because I had food in my hand most of the night."

"Don't do that," she says.

"Do what?"

"Put yourself down. He likes you, Lucy. A lot. And you like him too. Everyone could see that. Even Will noticed it, and you know how clueless men are about that kind of stuff."

I still. "He did?"

"Oh, yeah. He said that Travis better watch out because if he made a move on you, he'd be there to straighten him out. I was so jealous! I think it's cute how Will feels so protective of you. Like a big brother."

I feel horrible. I have to tell Brittany what's really going on between me and Will, but now isn't the time. I just hope she doesn't hate me when she finds out the truth.

Funny, a few months ago, I wouldn't have cared how Brittany felt about me. But now ... Will is still my best friend, but Brittany somehow managed to become my best girlfriend, and the thought of losing her friendship makes my stomach queasy.

"What do I do now?" Brittany asks. "About tonight?"

"Like I said, just act normal. You're supposed to go to the book club meeting, right? So show up at seven like everyone else and play along."

"Play along," she repeats intently. "Got it." She gives me another hug for good measure before taking off in her car.

I look down at Paco. "We're in a bit of a mess, aren't we? With this whole Travis, Will and Brittany thing?"

He makes a face that says, *I told you so*.

"You did not tell me so."

He barks and wags his tail in response.

This is insane. I think I'm having a conversation with my dog.

Brittany isn't the only one who needs a reality check.

I make one more attempt to get in touch with Will, but he's still not answering his phone, and he's not at home either. He hasn't changed his mind, has he?

No. Of course not. Will is coming to the book club meeting tonight to straighten out this mess. I know he is.

It's only five thirty, so I'm early, but it doesn't hurt to get a jump start. Since there will be lots of people attending tonight, which means lots of cars, I park my VW bug around the corner so that I don't take up a premium parking space that someone else might need. Between Paco and the muffins, I'll have to make two trips, but that's okay because it's a crisp, cool afternoon. No sweating from the car to the door today for anyone. I'm not sure what Betty Jean will make of me bringing Paco along to the meeting, but tough. If I'm forced to be the help tonight, then I'm bringing my dog.

I clip the leash to Paco's collar and pull a container of muffins from the back seat, balancing it carefully so that they don't get jostled because, trust me, there's absolutely nothing worse than a bruised muffin.

Paco and I walk on the sidewalk, admiring the houses that have been decorated for the holidays. Betty Jean lives in an older neighborhood composed of modest homes. But the lush gardens and pretty little white picket fences, along with the location, just a block from the gulf, make it prime real estate. I've only been to her house a couple of times, but even if I hadn't, it wouldn't be hard to figure out which one is hers because right there in her front lawn is a professionally made sign that says BETTY JEAN'S BOOK CLUB MEETS TONIGHT!

Paco and I grin at each other. Even though Betty Jean might get on my nerves at times (okay, a lot of the time), I can't help but admire her tenacity. Sure, she got the wrong J.W. Quicksilver to Whispering Bay. And yeah, he's a con man who has probably ripped off who knows how many people, but if it wasn't for her, Will wouldn't be stepping up to the plate tonight and telling everyone who he really is. So, in effect, she really has brought the real J.W. Quicksilver to town. Just not the way she thinks she has, but it will be the end result people remember about tonight.

I knock on the door and wait for her to answer. After a couple of minutes, I knock again. Knowing Betty Jean, she's probably still primping. I really hope she's ditched the seventies wig.

Paco starts whining. "Don't tell me you have to pee again?"

He looks up at me with those soulful brown eyes of his.

"Oh, all right." I unclip his leash. "Go do your thing. Just not on the sign," I tease. But instead of sniffing around in the front yard, Paco takes off like a bat out of hell and disappears from my sight.

Great. Just what I need. He probably thinks this is a game. I place the container with the muffins on a rocking chair on Betty Jean's front porch because now I have to chase my dog. "Paco! What's wrong with the yard in front?" I demand, following him around to the back of the house.

Only I don't see where he's gone. "Paco!" I yell.

The sound of familiar whimpering hits my ears. I've heard that sound before. And it's never been good. My mouth goes dry.

I find Paco hovering near the back door. His eyes are glazed, and he's panting. What's he seeing or hearing that I don't? There's a note taped to the door. With a hand that's already shaking, I take it down and read:

Lucy, I went to the Piggly Wiggly to get more wine. The door is open so go ahead and start setting up! BJ.

I turn the knob, and sure enough the door is unlocked. "You with me?" I ask Paco.

His eyes are so big, they look like they're going to explode out of this head. I step inside Betty Jean's kitchen. "Hello? Anybody home?" Other than an empty bottle of wine on the counter and two dirty glasses in the sink, the kitchen is obsessively neat, to the point that it could probably pass the white glove test.

Paco nudges me with his nose, then dashes off into the next room.

I take a deep breath and force my wobbly legs to follow. If my history with Paco repeats itself, I'm pretty sure what I'll find. I'm just not sure who it will be.

I walk into the quiet living room. Paco sits calmly at the foot of a lounge chair where a man is slumped over. My first reaction is intense relief that's it not Betty Jean. There's blood on the man's shirt. A quick inspection of the surroundings reveals a knife (Ugh! My least favorite murder weapon) lying on the coffee table in the center of the room.

I check the man's pulse. Nothing. His skin feels cool to the touch, and he's not breathing.

Paco slumps to the ground and begins to whine.

I reach into my pocket and retrieve my cell phone. Travis answers on the first ring. "Lucy, I'm glad you called. I just heard back from Agent Billings. You were right. That wasn't J.W. Quicksilver we saw last night. His name is Jefferson Pike, and he's wanted for questioning in at least three different con operations."

"Correction. The man's name *was* Jefferson Pike. I'm at Betty Jean's house. He's dead, Travis."

Chapter Ten

Betty Jean, Travis, Rusty Newton, three other cops, a fire truck and an ambulance, complete with screaming sirens and flashing lights, arrive on the scene at the same time. Paco and I meet them all at the door.

"What on earth! What's going on here? Why are all these people trying to get into my house?" Betty Jean stomps past me, takes one look at the body slumped in her living room chair, and stops cold. "Good gravy." She blinks. "He isn't dead, is he?"

"Actually, yeah," I say.

She sucks in a breath. "Heart attack?"

"Looks like he took a knife in the chest."

"Huh, what do you know? I told the Neighborhood Watch they needed to up their game, but does anyone ever listen to me?"

She starts to walk past the body, but Travis stops her. "Sorry," he says, "but we need to keep the area secure until we collect all the evidence."

One of the cops takes Betty Jean to sit inside a squad car until, as he puts it, "she calms down enough to answer questions." She seems pretty chill to me considering there's a dead body in her living room.

Travis waits until Betty Jean and the cop are out of earshot. "Are you all right?" he asks, his gaze full of concern. "Do you need to sit down? How about a glass of water?"

I think Travis has me confused with someone else. "That's sweet, but first things first. You need to arrest Hoyt Daniels or whatever his real name is. He was in on the con with Jefferson. The assistant ... Anita. She was probably in on it too. They can't leave town, Travis."

Now that he's reminded that I'm no shrinking violet, he goes back into cop mode. "Let the police take care of that. Tell me everything that happened once you got here. And don't leave out any details."

I tell him everything that went down, including finding the note on the back door. He asks me to retrace my steps, so I show him how I opened the door, then looked around the kitchen and eventually went into the living room. "And you got here around five thirty?" he asks.

"Yes."

"What made you go into the living room?"

"You won't like it."

"Try me."

"Paco led me into the house. He knew there was a dead body inside. And exactly where it was."

"Because he's a ghost whisperer?"

"Because he's ... something. Except a cadaver dog. We know he's not one of those."

Travis's expression turns grim. "Do you mind waiting outside while we finish up in here? I have more questions, but I want to make sure the crime scene guys get everything."

I wish I could take a walk around the block to let go of all this adrenaline inside, but the street is closed off. There's already a crowd gathered behind the barricades. Paco is in the front yard with Rusty. I take over dog-watching duty and join Betty Jean, who's sitting in the back of a police car, drinking coffee.

"Are you okay?" I ask her.

The Farrah Fawcett wig sits crooked, and her mascara is smeared. Tears? From Betty Jean? I put my arm around her. "This must be a shock."

"I'll say. Do you know how much your property devalues in price when people find out there's been a murder in the house?"

O-kay. Good to know some things never change.

She looks at me. "Maybe ... I'm in a little bit of shock," she admits. "I was only gone thirty minutes. When I left, he was very much alive, believe me." She takes a sip of her coffee. "I overheard the cops say that he isn't really J.W. Quicksilver."

"His name is Jefferson Pike. And he's a con man."

She snorts. "Figures."

"What was he doing here? I thought the book club meeting didn't start until seven."

"He came over early to set up."

The hair on my neck stands on end. "Oh yeah?"

Her blue eyes harden. "That's my story, and I'm sticking to it."

"Is that what you plan to tell the police?"

"Yep."

Whatever Jefferson Pike was doing here two hours before book club, it sure as heck wasn't helping Betty Jean "set up." I try to think of a way to ask her what I want to know without hurting her pride. Since Betty Jean isn't easily offended, I go the blunt route.

"Jefferson Pike was running a con. He and another man named Hoyt Daniels, although that's probably not his real name, were swindling people out of money and promising them that J.W. Quicksilver was going to publish their books." I pause. "Is that what he promised you? Because if it was, there's no shame in that. He was good. They both were. According to Travis, the FBI was looking into him for three other con schemes."

Betty Jean looks amused. "What do you take me for? I'm no schmuck. No one's swindling me out of any of my ex-husbands' hard-earned money."

Emphasis on ex-husbands *plural*. Betty Jean doesn't mind telling you that she's been married and divorced four times. She's also telling the truth. She never gave Jefferson Pike any money.

Rusty taps on the car window. "Are you all right to answer questions now, Betty Jean?"

"Right as I'll ever be." She pats my hand on the way out of the car. "Looks like you won't need to serve tonight after all. But I still want the muffins you brought. I can freeze them for next week's book club."

Right.

With Betty Jean back in the house, I walk over toward the barricade. My parents, as well as the rest of the book club members, are on the other side. "Lucy! What's going on? Are you okay?" Mom asks. "Is it true? Is J.W. Quicksilver—I mean, is that man dead?" Apparently, word has gotten out on the street that the man they all came to see wasn't J.W. Quicksilver but an impostor.

"I'm fine. And yes, he's dead. But until Travis gives me permission, I can't say much else."

Dad shakes his head. "Horrible. The crime in this town is reaching epidemic proportions. And to think, we used to be the Safest City in America," he says, referring to the city's tagline. He has a point.

"Lucy!" Brittany pushes her way to the front of the crowd. "What's going on? I hear there's been a murder!" She lowers her voice. "Where's the real J.W. Quicksilver? Didn't you tell me he was going to be here tonight?"

"I have no idea where he is, but ... yeah, he'll be here. He promised."

"Who is he?" she demands.

"Not now, Brittany."

She makes a huffing sound. "Then when?"

"I promise you, once you find out who it is, this will all make sense."

A woman in the crowd taps Brittany on the shoulder, and they engage in conversation.

Victor Marino and I exchange glances. He looks worried. Not that I blame him. Now that Jefferson Pike is dead, everything about his con scheme will come out, including the victims he swindled. I hope the police can recoup his money.

My cell phone rings. It's Will!

"Where have you been? I've been calling you all day."

"It's a long story."

"I'm listening."

"Not on the phone." He sounds tense. "Can you come over to my place?'

"Not until the police tell me I can leave."

"Leave where? Lucy, what's going on?"

"The guy who's been impersonating you? His name was Jefferson Pike. And he's dead."

"Dead?" There's a pause. "How?"

"He was stabbed in the chest. Paco and I found him at Betty Jean's house. Speaking of which, aren't you supposed to be here for your big coming-out party? What happened?"

"That's part of the long story. I'm on my way to the police station to talk to the cops."

My Spidey sense shakes a tambourine in my face. If I've learned anything in these past couple of months, it's that I should listen to it. "No, don't go to the cops. Not until we have a chance to talk first."

"But—"

"Promise me," I add firmly.

We make plans to meet up later tonight, then hang up. Rusty hands me a cup of coffee. I take a deep, appreciative sip. "Thanks. I needed that. Can you thank the Good Samaritan who provided this?"

"You can thank her yourself." He points to the other side of the barricade, where Heidi Burrows stands behind a card table handing out doughnuts and cups of coffee.

She's shameless. She really is. I suppose this is more of her "community relations" program. This coffee doesn't taste nearly as good as it did a few seconds ago.

Heidi spots me and waves. I have no choice but to wave back. "Thanks for the coffee," I call out.

She makes a thumbs-up gesture.

Ugh. I wish I could take a much-needed walk around the block, but I can't leave until the cops okay it. Paco nudges my leg with his nose. He has his *I need to do my business* look.

"You want some privacy?"

He barks once, which we've pretty much established means yes.

I walk him over by the side of the house near a row of hibiscus bushes. It's dark now, so the motion detector lights come on. A lizard pops its head out of a gutter. Paco goes after him, but of course, the lizard retreats inside. He repeats this jack-in-the-box routine, popping his head in and out, then scurrying back into the pipe. Paco totally falls for it, whining and pawing at the gutter. For the world's smartest dog, he sure can be dumb sometimes.

"Paco, leave that lizard alone." Still, I let this continue for a few minutes because everyone deserves a guilty pleasure now and then. "Okay, that's enough. Let's—" Something shiny catches my eye. I bend over and scoop it up from the grass.

It's an earring. A big one. Betty Jean must have lost it while gardening. An image of Betty Jean all decked out in her Farrah Fawcett wig and these earrings makes me smile. I slip the earring into the pocket of my jeans.

"There you are. I've been looking for you."

I jump at the sound of Travis's voice. I must be more spooked than I realized. "I was just taking Paco for a walk. Is it okay if I go now?" *Because I really need to talk to Will and find out where he's been all day.*

"Do you mind if we do one more walk through the house?"

I reenact everything, starting with finding the note taped to the back door, walking through the kitchen, and then finally into the living room. They've taken Jefferson Pike's body out of the house. Bloodstains mar the chair and the carpet, making it look like a set right out of a slasher film. I really hope those stains come out.

"Where's Betty Jean?" I ask. "Still outside with Rusty?"

"I believe so."

"The knife? Did it come from her kitchen?"

"Looks that way," says Travis. "There's no defense wounds on Pike's body, and from the way his body was found lying on the chair, it looks like whoever did this took him completely by surprise. He might have even been asleep when he was stabbed."

I turn to stare at him. I'm pretty sure my jaw must be on the floor.

"What?" he says.

"I can't believe you just told me all that. Don't you remember our first murder investigation?" I deepen my voice to imitate him. "Sorry, ma'am, I can't answer those kinds of questions."

"I guess I was kind of a jerk, huh?"

"Just a little."

We smile, then we remember where we are and what we're doing, and the mood turns somber. My bladder takes a moment to remind me of something else as well. "Do you mind if I go to the bathroom? I promise not to touch anything."

"Sure," says Travis. "The rooms have all been cleared."

I head down the hallway and open the first door on the right, but it's not the bathroom. A pair of walking shoes is arranged neatly in front of a closet door. I recognize them. They're Betty Jean's. This must be her bedroom. And like the rest of the house, it's obsessively tidy.

Except one thing. The bed is unmade, and the sheets are rumpled.

An image so disturbing pops into my head that I have to immediately block it out, otherwise my brain might explode.

Betty Jean and Jefferson Pike? No! But then ... why not? She's only about fifteen years older than him, and she's been looking mighty sassy lately. I always thought her aggressive cougar routine was just that—a routine. Clearly, I've been naïve.

After I finish up in the bathroom, Travis secures the house. The barricades have been taken down and the crowds are mostly gone. So is Heidi and her impromptu "coffee stand."

Rusty tells Travis that he needs to call the police station ASAP. "I'll be right back after I take this call," he tells me.

Betty Jean finishes up a conversation with one of the crime scene guys, then turns to look at her house with a bleak expression. Not that I blame her. The yellow crime tape plastered over her front door serves as a not-so-subtle reminder of what happened here this evening.

"They said I can come back tomorrow afternoon," she says.

"Where will you go tonight?"

"Panama City. There's a hotel on the beach that still has those vibrating beds." She wags her brows up and down.

The idea of Betty Jean driving forty-five minutes to Panama City and spending the night all alone in a seedy motel is depressing. She has friends, but I don't see her asking any of them if she can crash at their place. She's too stubborn and independent for that.

I can't believe what I'm about to do.

"Well, I just hope I can get some sleep tonight. I'll tell you a secret. I hate living all alone. The thought of going back to that big, empty apartment ... " I shudder dramatically. "It's times like this I wish I had a roommate."

"Try melatonin," says Betty Jean. "Or whiskey. Either one does the trick every time."

Looks like I'll have to try the direct approach again. "Want to spend the night at my place? I could use the company."

She ponders this a moment. "Why not?" Then her eyes narrow. "You don't snore, do you?"

"Not that I'm aware of, but it doesn't matter. I have a guest bedroom. You're more than welcome to it. For as long as you need."

"Let me see if I can sweet-talk one of those cops into letting me back in the house to grab my toothbrush. I'll meet you at your place." She struts over to talk to a police officer.

Travis stops me on the way to my car. "I just got off the phone with the station. Normally, I wouldn't share this with anyone, but since you're the one who tipped us off about Jefferson Pike, I thought you'd like to know that about an hour ago we caught Hoyt Daniels and Anita Tremble. They were outside of Tallahassee when they got stopped by the highway patrol for a broken taillight. Lucky for us, the officer noticed we'd just put out an APB on them. They're being brought to Whispering Bay for questioning."

"Good. Are you going to arrest Hoyt for Pike's murder?"

"His name isn't Hoyt Daniels. It's Archie Clements. According to the FBI database, he's a person of interest in the same cons they were looking at Pike for."

"What about Anita Tremble?"

"It looks like she just joined the gang a few months ago. No alias on her that we can find."

"Not yet anyway. So, you've got the killer. Right? You're probably going to find Archie Clements's fingerprints all over Betty Jean's house."

"The knife was wiped clean." Travis blows out a breath. "You're not going to believe what Clements is saying."

"Oh, I'm sure he's going around screaming that he's innocent."

"Naturally. But he's also giving us the name of the murderer too."

I laugh incredulously. "I bet. Who's the poor dupe he's trying to pin it on?"

"J.W. Quicksilver."

I feel the blood drain from my face. Luckily, it's dark outside so Travis won't notice. "What?"

"He says the real J.W. Quicksilver came to see Pike this afternoon, and the two of them had it out. As goofy as his story sounds, it actually makes sense. Quicksilver had a motive. Pike was using his name to swindle people. Now we need to find out if this world-famous reclusive author had the opportunity."

"How ... I mean, does Clements know where to find J.W. Quicksilver?"

"I'm on my way to police headquarters to find that out."

Chapter Eleven

I give Betty Jean the keys to The Bistro and tell her to "knock herself out," then Paco and I hightail it straight to Will's. I get there to find Will lying on the couch holding a bag of frozen peas to his head. Underneath the bag of peas is a lump the size of a walnut.

"Holy wow, what happened?"

"I got knocked over the head."

"By who?"

"Jefferson Pike."

"I think you better start from the beginning. Wait. Better yet, let's get you to a hospital. You can tell me the story in the car."

Like a typical man, Will blows off his injury. "I don't need to go to the hospital."

"No one's asking you. You're getting that lump checked out and that's that."

After all our years together, he knows better than to argue with me. We leave Paco back at his place. If Will had a TV, I'd put on Animal Planet (Paco's favorite channel), but Will doesn't own a set, so Paco will have to make do with a bowl of water and a blanket for company.

It's a forty-five-minute drive to the nearest hospital, which gives me more than plenty of time to hear this story. Since Will is in no condition to drive, we take my car.

"Ever since you told me about the publishing scam, I haven't been able to think straight," says Will. "I decided I didn't want to wait until the book club meeting to tell everyone the truth. My plan was to go directly to the cops."

"Good idea. What stopped you?"

"Too-stupid-to-live syndrome. I figured that once I went to the cops and they arrested Pike, he'd probably clam up and I wouldn't get the answers I needed, so I decided to confront him first."

"You went to confront a potentially dangerous con man? All by yourself? You're right. You are too stupid to live," I say, feeling a fresh spurt of anger come on. "He could have killed you."

"I told you, I wasn't thinking straight. All I could think of was that this guy was using my name and my reputation as an author to dupe innocent people out of their hard-earned money. And then when Brittany told me how the chamber of commerce was comping a beach house for Pike and his accomplices—"

"Archie Clements and Anita. Travis told me they're both in custody and that Archie is claiming that you killed Jefferson Pike."

"Me? I've been tied up in a closet for the past four hours. I haven't had time to kill anyone. Although I admit, I would have enjoyed wringing that bastard's neck."

"You better not let anyone hear you say that. Besides, someone with a penchant for knives beat you to it."

"Was the crime scene gruesome?"

Will knows that my least favorite episodes of *America's Most Vicious Criminals* are the ones that involve stabbings. "Strangely enough, it wasn't too bad. Whoever did it aimed right for the heart. It looks like they used a knife from Betty Jean's kitchen, wiped it clean of prints, then left it behind on the coffee table."

"Definitely a crime of passion."

"My money is on Archie. He's the partner. I bet Jefferson was planning to double-cross him by stealing the money and running off to South America." Out of the corner of my eye, I see Will sporting a grin. "Hey. It happens on TV all the time."

Will gets serious. "Yeah, but I can't imagine that they'd make that much money off this scam. They were only going to be in town, what? A couple of days? Let's say they managed to get ten victims at a few thousand bucks each. That kind of money is hardly worth the effort."

"To you it's not, Mr. Fancy Rich Author, but ten or twenty thousand dollars to someone like me? That's a lot of money." My cell phone pings. I glance at my screen. It's Betty Jean. "What does she want?" I mutter.

Will follows my gaze. "Why is Betty Jean Collins calling you at ten o'clock at night?"

I put the phone on speaker. "Hey, Betty Jean. Everything all right?"

"Where are you? I'm bored. I've already searched through all your drawers and closets."

I can't very well tell Betty Jean that I'm taking Will to the hospital because then she'd ask a lot of questions, and I'd either have to lie to her or drag her into our mess. Besides, I have a feeling that when it comes to Jefferson Pike, she might have her own bit of a mess to worry about.

"I'm ... at Will's. We're working on a crossword puzzle together and we can't stop until we finish. So don't wait up. This could take a while. And please stop going through my things, okay?"

Betty Jean chuckles. "Crossword puzzle, huh? Is that what your generation calls it? Oh well. You said to knock myself out. Does that include the mac and cheese in your fridge?"

"You can have anything you want," I say, desperate to end this conversation.

"Okey-doke. Say hi to Will for me. Good luck with that puzzle," she says before hanging up.

Will raises an amused brow. "Crossword puzzle?"

"Since everyone in town knows that you don't own a TV, I couldn't very well tell her that we were watching a movie. It was the first thing off the top of my head."

"I'm afraid to ask, but what's Betty Jean doing at your place?"

"A man was murdered in her house. She was going to go to some fleabag motel for the night. I couldn't let her be alone."

"You're a nice person, Lucy."

"You would have done the same thing."

"Not if it was Betty Jean Collins."

I can't help but grin. "Okay, back to your story. You confronted Jefferson Pike at the beach house. Then what?"

"I told him I was J.W. Quicksilver. It never occurred to him that the real J.W. would show up. At first, he didn't believe me, but then I proved it to him."

"How did you do that?"

"I pulled out my phone and showed him a couple of emails from my publisher."

"I bet he laid an egg."

"Pretty much." Will gets quiet. "I asked him why of all the authors in the world he picked me for this scam. And you want to know what he said? He said it was because I'd made it so easy for him. By being anonymous I was practically *begging* for something like this to happen. He said I deserved it."

"That must have made you mad."

"Yeah." He blows out a breath. "This is where the too-stupid-to-live part comes into play. I told him I was going straight to the police and there was nothing he could do to stop me."

I moan. "You never tell the bad guy that you're going to turn them in to the police. That's like something straight out of a bad James Bond movie."

"First off, there's no such thing as a bad James Bond movie. And tell me about it. The next thing I knew, I was tied up in a closet with the worst hangover of my life."

"How did you get out?"

"After a few hours, I was able to loosen the ropes. I thought about calling the police right away, but I called you instead."

"Was there anyone else at the beach house? Did you see Archie or Anita?"

"Just Pike. If anyone else was there, they didn't show themselves."

None of this makes sense. I try to put myself in Jefferson Pike's head. "Okay, so you go to see Pike, and you tell him the truth. So now he knows the jig's up and he's going to be exposed. He hits you over the head, ties you up and drags you into a closet. Why not skip town then? Why still go to Betty Jean's house for the book club meeting and risk getting arrested?"

"Maybe he was still waiting to collect money from some of his victims? Maybe he thought I wouldn't be able to escape? Who knows how this sociopath thinks?"

"He must have told Archie about you, because Archie told the cops that you killed Jefferson."

Will drags a hand down his face. "What a mess. I wish I'd listened to you and exposed the guy last night at The Harbor House. Now he's dead, and his partner is trying to pin the murder on me."

"Except ... I wonder if Archie knows who you are."

"What do you mean?"

"I mean, Jefferson Pike knows you as J.W. Quicksilver, but does he know that you're Will Cunningham?"

Will thinks on it. "Now that you mention it, I never gave him my name. I just walked in guns blazing and told him I was the real J.W. Quicksilver."

"You stood up at the reading to ask him a question." I think back to last night. "I'm pretty sure Brittany introduced you as the town's head librarian."

"Maybe Pike didn't remember that detail? There were a lot of people at The Harbor House last night."

"Let's assume for now that Pike just told Archie that the real J.W. is here in town, but he never told him your real name because he doesn't know it. That would mean that Archie would have no idea who you were or how to find you."

"You know what they say about assumptions, Lucy."

"There's an easy way to figure it out."

"How?"

"If Archie Clements knows that Will Cunningham is the real J.W. Quicksilver and he's told the cops that you're a murderer, then I expect that someone from the Whispering Bay Police Department will be paying you a visit soon."

We arrive at the ER, where Will is diagnosed with a mild concussion. Four hours later, he's discharged with instructions to be monitored closely. I volunteer to spend what's left of the night at his place to make sure that he's okay.

We pull up to an empty house. "Well, at least the cops aren't waiting on my doorstep to arrest me."

"Or they just got tired and left and they'll be back first thing in the morning."

"How about I beat them to the punch and go down to talk to them before they come to talk to me?"

"It's the responsible thing to do," I agree.

He turns in his seat to face me. "I know this is asking a lot, but will you come with me to the station? For moral support?"

"I'm your best friend. Of course, I'll come with you."

"Thanks, Lucy. You're the best."

I hesitate, because this is probably the worst possible time to drop this on him, but I have to know. "Why didn't you trust me? Why didn't you tell me that you were J.W. Quicksilver? You told Sebastian, but you didn't tell me."

"I'm sorry. I should have told you, but it had nothing to do with trust, because I do trust you." He looks at me oddly. "Honestly? I thought it was weird that you didn't figure it out on your own. Lucy, do you know how many times I've lied to you about it?"

Bunches, I bet. Time for my own confession. "I've never caught you in a lie. Not until that night we kissed and I asked you outright if you were J.W. Quicksilver."

"Never?" he asks incredulously.

"Never. I think it was because ... you know, my feelings for you got in the way or something."

"About those feelings—"

"Can we talk about this later? When we don't have to worry about running from the law?"

"We're going to run from the law?"

"If we have to."

He grins.

"Let's get in the house and get some sleep. I'll set my alarm to wake you up in an hour."

He moans. "Do we really have to do that?"

"Doctor's orders," I say in a fake cheery voice.

I hunker down in Will's guest room, exhausted but too wound up to sleep right away. Like I told Will, going to the police is the right thing to do. But despite the fact that he hasn't done anything illegal, I can't help but feel that J.W. Quicksilver is in a whole heap of trouble.

Chapter Twelve

I WAKE UP FEELING like something is wrong. A shaft of light streams through the window hitting me in the—*light*? I jump up from the bed and pull back the blinds. The sun is shining like it's daytime. Getting up at four every morning to make the muffins means it's always dark outside. I grab my cell phone. It's seven in the morning!

Paco jumps on the bed and licks my face.

"Why didn't you wake me up at the regular time?" I demand.

He makes a sorry face, but I can tell he doesn't really mean it.

I immediately text Sarah. **I can't believe I overslept. I'm on my way**!

After a few minutes, she texts back. **No worries. We have everything under control. You just stay where you are**. This is followed by a winking smiley face. Huh. That's weird.

Oh no. I hope Betty Jean didn't tell Sarah that Will and I were "putting together a puzzle" last night.

I slip on my sneakers, brush my teeth, and grab Paco's leash. Will walks into the living room and yawns. "What time is it?" he asks, looking adorably sleepy.

"Better yet, what year is it?" I should probably check his pupils too.

"The year of owning up to being J.W. Quicksilver," he shoots back.

"Good enough. I guess you're not going to slip into a coma."

He watches me dash around the living room trying to find my purse. "I thought we were going to the police station together this morning."

I stop scrambling and turn to face him. "Yeah, about that ... I've been thinking."

"Oh no," he mutters.

"Hear me out."

"With no caffeine in my system? No, thanks."

Excellent idea. I finish getting ready while Will makes the coffee. He hands me a mug and orders me to sit on the couch. "Okay, I'm ready now. Go."

"Don't you think it's weird that the cops haven't come by or called you yet? They've had Archie Clements in custody since last night. If he told Travis that you're the real J.W. Quicksilver, Travis would have come here by now. Or, at the very least, called you."

Will takes a long sip of his coffee. "I was thinking the same thing myself."

"Let's say you go down to the police station and tell everyone that you're the real J.W. How long do you think before the rest of the world finds out?" Before Will can answer, I tell him. "Maybe a day or two at most. If you're lucky."

"I told you. I'm ready to let everyone know who I am."

"Sure. If this was a book signing or a release party or some big article in *People* magazine, it would be great. But the first thing everyone is going to associate with your coming out is that you're a suspect in a murder case. How do you think book sales are going to do?"

"Honestly? I'm just jaded enough to think that it probably won't matter. It might even help sales. The world is a kooky place, Lucy."

"True. But what about your reputation? You said you wanted to come out on your own terms. I don't think this is what you meant by that."

"Once the cops know I've got an alibi for the time of the murder, I'll be off the hook. Remember I was knocked out and tied up in a closet?"

"Says you. Do you have any proof of that?"

"I've got a lump on my noggin."

"That we told the doctor at the hospital came from a bowling ball that fell off a garage shelf and landed on your head. Which, by the way—quick thinking." At the time at least. In retrospect, maybe we should have told the truth, but if we had, the cops would have gotten involved, and last night we weren't ready for that. "You said there was no one else at the house when you got there. The only person who knows you were left in that closet is you and Jefferson Pike. And he isn't talking. At least not without the help of The Sunshine Ghost Society and a seance."

Will snorts, but I can see that I'm getting through to him. "So what now?" he asks. "Just sit back and let my name be dragged through the mud? If I don't clear myself, then this Clements guy is going to keep telling everyone that J.W. Quicksilver killed Jefferson Pike."

"Not if I find out who the real killer is."

Paco barks happily.

"See, Paco agrees with me."

"I don't know, Lucy. This all seems a bit harebrained to me."

"Last night you said you trusted me. Was that just lip service?"

His eyes flash angrily. "No."

"Then trust me to find who killed Jefferson Pike. Then, when I find the real killer, you can let the world know who you are because you want to. Not because you're being forced."

I dash into the café's kitchen. "I'm here!"

Jill looks up from the sink and grins at me. "Long night?"

Sarah, who's manning the counter, pops her head through the pass-through window into the kitchen. "I told you there was no need to rush. We're handling everything fine between the three of us."

The three of us?

At the confused look on my face, Sarah nods toward the dining room. "Go take a look. She's fabulous!"

I walk out to see Betty Jean serving table four near the window. She's wearing a pair of jeans and a T-shirt that says, JUST A MUFFIN LOOKING FOR HER STUD.

"Oh, my ... " Nothing else comes out of my mouth.

Betty Jean is wearing my T-shirt, strutting around the café and chitchatting with customers like it's something she does every day.

"When I got here this morning, she'd already made the coffee," says Sarah. "There's no fresh muffins, but I offered the customers who complained half price off their orders, and everyone seemed happy enough."

Betty Jean trots over. "Well, well, well. Look what the cat dragged in." She looks me up and down. "Isn't that the same thing you had on last night?"

Sarah tries not to laugh.

"Yes, but it's not what you think," I say with as much dignity as I can muster. "Thanks for helping out, but I'm here now. You can go upstairs and take a nap."

"Why? I'm not tired."

"You don't mind staying?" Sarah asks Betty Jean. "Because I actually have something I need to do."

"Go!" Betty Jean waves her off. "I've got this."

She's got this? What? Betty Jean has been working here all of two hours, and now she's an expert. But if Sarah has something to do, I don't want to be the one to keep her from it. It's too busy this morning to run the café with just Jill and I, so I'm going to have to give in here and let Betty Jean stay.

"Okay," I relent. "Thanks, Betty Jean. Just try your best." I take my position behind the counter. Jill puts a completed order up on the pass-through. Betty Jean looks at the ticket, picks up the tray, and delivers it to the correct table. Then she goes around the room offering coffee refills.

"I told you," Sarah says, following my stunned gaze. "Betty Jean is terrific. Maybe we should think about hiring her a few mornings a week."

"Do you want to stay in business?"

"I admit, she can be salty sometimes, but I think the customers might actually like it. She'd add a dash of flavor, that's for sure."

"We'll see."

Sarah hesitates. "You know, Lucy, just because we've always done things one way doesn't mean we can't change it up every now and then. A successful business stays flexible so it can react to the market."

Where have I heard this before? I place my brain on overtime, and then it comes to me. It's the same exact thing Heidi said to me the other day. Weird.

"I heard about this Jefferson Pike person being found dead." Sarah shudders. "The customers have been talking about it nonstop. Unbelievable, huh? How he was impersonating J.W. Quicksilver. Poor Betty Jean. I can't imagine how traumatic this has been for her. It was nice of you to let her stay here last night. Speaking of which ... what's going on with you and Will?"

"Not what you think is going on. It's a long story, and as soon as I can, I'll tell you everything."

Sarah makes a disappointed face. "I guess I'll have to wait until then." She pulls her purse from behind the counter. "You're really okay with me leaving for the day?"

"How many times have you covered for me? Yes. Go. Have fun. Or whatever."

The next hour goes by quickly. I try to concentrate on taking orders, all the while thinking of how I'm going to find Jefferson Pike's murderer, when Anita Tremble walks into the café. Paco sits up at attention.

"I thought you were in jail," I say.

"I'm not the one who takes photos they're not supposed to."

Oh? She wants attitude. I'll give her attitude. "How does it feel to know that you're responsible for milking innocent people out of their hard-earned money?"

Her face falls. "I won't pretend I'm innocent. I knew about the scam. But this was my first time. That's why I'm out on bail."

At least she doesn't have the gall to lie to me about it. "What are you doing here?" I ask.

"Trying to get breakfast. I spent the night in jail, and I'm hungry." She still has that mousy look about her, but in the clear daylight, I notice how young she is. Pretty, too.

"How old are you?" I ask.

"Twenty-five."

"Look, it's none of my business what you do with your life, but if this really was your first sting operation, maybe you can turn things around."

"My attorney says that since I don't have a record and that my involvement was minimal, I might get off with probation. But Archie won't be that lucky." Her voice goes shaky with emotion. "The FBI is coming to town to question him about a bunch of stuff he and Jefferson were into. He's not a bad person. Not really. He just got involved with the wrong man."

"Jefferson Pike."

Anita nods. "He was bad news. I see that now."

It occurs to me that Anita could be a terrific source of information. I need to find out exactly what she knows. There's no one in line behind her, and Betty Jean does seem to have the swing of things. "It sounds like you've been through a lot. Can I buy you breakfast?"

She perks up. "Really? That's so sweet of you." She orders a breakfast sandwich and a coffee, and I throw in a banana walnut muffin on the side.

I hand her the coffee and pour one of my own. "Do you mind if I join you?"

"Sure, why not?"

Betty Jean is busy refilling napkin holders. I tap her on the shoulder. "I know I just got here, but I need to take a break. Do you think you can handle the counter for a few minutes?"

"Put the order in the computer, let Jill cook it up, then serve it. Piece of cake."

"Sarah showed you how to use the computer?"

"Why is it you millennials think you're the only ones who can do technology? Of course I can use the computer."

"Okay, thanks. Holler if you need me." I bend down to whisper to Paco, "Stay here and keep an eye on her." He wags his tail.

Under Paco's direction, I leave Betty Jean to "do" technology and follow Anita to the dining area.

Even though there are empty tables near the window that faces the gulf, she gravitates to the back of the café. Poor kid. She probably doesn't want anyone to notice her. Not that I blame her. This is a small town. Who knows how many people Jefferson Pike swindled? If I were her, I'd want to get out of Whispering Bay as fast as I could.

I wait till she's had a sip of her coffee before saying, "You know that Archie is claiming that the real J.W. Quicksilver is the one who killed Jefferson?"

"Talk about ironic," she says.

"I know," I say, playing along to get her trust. "Completely crazy! How did it happen? I mean, did he just show up and say, 'I'm the real J.W. Quicksilver' or what?"

"Not exactly." She wiggles around in her seat. "Look, Lucy, you seem like a nice person, but I'm not sure how much I should tell you. My attorney said I needed to be discreet."

"Oh, I can be discreet. I'm just trying to wrap my head around what happened. The whole town is. If we could only understand how this all went down." I sigh dramatically. "That Jefferson Pike, he was a real charmer, wasn't he? I bet he wasn't even Scottish."

"No, he wasn't."

I knew it!

"How did you get involved with him?"

"Archie. He and I became ... friends. Jefferson and Archie have been partners for, like, ten years. They'd been running real estate scams all along the east coast and were making their way down to Key West, but Jefferson was always on the lookout for a quick buck. When he ran into Betty Jean Collins on an online reader board asking if anyone could get in touch with J.W. Quicksilver, it was too good for him to pass up. Jefferson is, I mean … was a huge fan of his books and he thought it would be cool to impersonate his idol. They needed a third person, so they reached out to me to help with the con."

"And you've never done anything like this before?"

Her eyes get teary. "Never. I know I shouldn't have gotten involved, but once I met Jefferson, it was hard to say no to him. I lost my job a few months ago, and he made it sound so easy. The plan was to stay in town a couple of days, then split the money. Archie and Jefferson would go on to Key West, and I'd go back to Jersey. That's where I'm from."

The hair on my neck tingles. I've just caught Anita in a lie. Only I'm not sure which part of what she's just said to me isn't true. Or maybe the whole thing isn't true. Ack. This is where things can get muddy. I need to keep my questions simple.

"So did you actually see the real J.W. Quicksilver?"

"No. Archie and I were out collecting money. When we got back to the beach house, Jefferson told us that the real J.W. Quicksilver was in town and that he was going to expose us to the police."

"You must have been terrified."

"Oh! I was. So was Archie. We'd … I'm ashamed to admit this, but we'd gotten almost thirty thousand in cash on the swindle already. It was more than enough for me and Archie. We wanted to cut our losses and leave town before the real J.W. Quicksilver could get to the cops."

"But it wasn't enough money for Jefferson, was it?"

"The money was never an issue. It was the game. Jefferson really got his kicks playing the famous author. It was his ego that got him killed."

There's anger in her voice. I think back to the night of the reading and I get it. The smug confidence, the Scottish accent, not to mention that ridiculous kilt of his. Jefferson Pike's ego must have been bigger than the Grand Canyon.

"I'm still confused. If the real J.W. Quicksilver was in town and he was going to the cops, what made Jefferson think he could still attend the book club meeting without getting caught?"

Anita glances around the table, then lowers her voice. "Jefferson told Archie that he hit J.W. Quicksilver over the head with a marble bookend. Then he tied him up and left him in a closet. I guess he thought he wouldn't be able to escape. But I swear, I didn't know about that until my lawyer told me last night. Archie was trying to protect me, so he kept that from me."

"So, did Archie see the real J.W. Quicksilver? Does he know who he is?" I hold my breath, waiting for her to answer.

"I don't know. Like I said, he didn't tell me any of that. Archie and Jefferson were the real team. I was just brought in to play a part for show. Archie tried to keep the details from me. In case we got caught. And now my attorney says I can't see Archie." She looks down at her plate. "I wish I knew how he was holding up. He's not a bad man. Not like Jefferson."

Everything Anita has just said is true. But I'm picking up on a lot of emotion here. Could Archie and Anita be involved? He's old enough to be her father, but it wouldn't be the world's first May-December romance.

I glance over to the counter, where a small line is forming. Betty Jean seems to have gotten the swing of things, but I should probably help her. I turn back to face Anita. She's gazing at Betty Jean with fury.

"What's that woman doing here?" she demands.

"Who? Betty Jean? She stayed here last night. Why, what's wrong?"

Anita shakes herself back in control. "I know it's irrational to blame her. But if she hadn't reached out on that message board trying to find

J.W. Quicksilver, Jefferson would have never had the idea to come here and play this con."

Talk about blaming the victim.

"Sorry. She must be your friend, huh? I didn't mean to overreact. It's been a rough twenty-four hours."

"What happens now?" I ask.

"They kicked me out of the beach house, so I'm in a cheap hotel until they figure out what to do with me. My lawyer says I can't leave town until the police and FBI say I can."

"Well, good luck. I better get back to work."

"Thanks. You've been real sweet to listen to me." On her way out the door, she turns to wave goodbye.

So that didn't provide much in the way of information.

It looks like the only person who can give me the answers that are going to help Will is Archie Clements. And he's sitting in the Whispering Bay jail waiting for the feds to come get him. Somehow, I need to find a way to get to him first.

Chapter Thirteen

I'VE HAD A FEW hours to think of a plan to get me inside the jail to talk to Archie Clements, but it's going to depend on a massive dose of luck. Hopefully, the sleuthing gods are with me today.

After the last customer leaves, I lock up. Since it's Jill's day to do final cleanup, I run upstairs to take a quick shower before heading down to the police station. Betty Jean follows me into the apartment.

"That went well, don't you think?"

"Actually, yeah. It did. Thanks, Betty Jean. You're a real lifesaver."

Her gaze follows me as I grab a clean set of clothes from my dresser. "Who would have thought you and I would be the same size?"

Yeah. About that. It's kind of creepy that she went through my stuff to get my T-shirt. But on the other hand, she was such a trooper about chipping in to help that I really can't complain.

"The same size on top, I mean. All your jeans are way too big for me in the butt. You know, there's exercises you can do to get rid of that. I still have an old Jane Fonda workout tape if you want to borrow it. Go for the burn!"

I honestly have no idea what to say to that.

"Of course, some men really like that extra junk in the trunk. Looks like you've found two of them. Well done! I didn't think you had it in you, but—"

"Betty Jean, do you mind? I'd rather not talk about my love life."

"Whatever you say. But if you ever want some man advice, I'm your girl. I managed to get four of 'em to the altar, you know."

And get divorced four times too. I wisely keep that statistic to myself.

"I was thinking," says Betty Jean. "The cops said I could go back to my house today, but I know you hate to be here all alone."

"No worries," I say quickly. "You've done enough already. I can manage."

"But why should you when I can stay longer? Besides, I got ripped off last night. I thought we were going to drink margaritas and give each other mani-pedis. Instead you spent the night with Will Cunningham." She tsks. "I never thought you were the type to choose bros over hoes."

I blink hard. "I think you've got that expression wrong."

"No, I don't. It means you picked a man over one of your girlfriends."

"No, it means ... oh, never mind. Sure, you can spend the night again."

"Great! I'll have dinner ready when you get home."

Oh boy.

I hop into the bathroom and start to undress when I discover an earring in the pocket of my jeans. I'd forgotten all about it. I stick my head out the bathroom door. "Hey, Betty Jean, I found your earring."

She comes over to look at the earring in my outstretched palm. "What made you think that gaudy piece of glass belongs to me?"

"I found it on the grass outside your house."

"Then it could belong to anyone."

"It was over by the hibiscus bushes. Beneath a window. Um, the second window back? I thought maybe you lost it while gardening."

She bends over to inspect it closer. "Oh. You're right. It is mine. Thanks, Lucy." She takes the earring from my hand and walks away, leaving the hair on my neck standing at attention.

On the way to police headquarters, I practice what I'm going to say to convince Travis to let me see Archie Clements. This isn't going to be easy to pull off. In fact, it's going to be downright impossible, but I have to try. My thoughts wander to Betty Jean and the earring. Why did she lie about it belonging to her? I shrug it off. Knowing Betty Jean, it could be any number of goofy reasons.

Paco and I walk into the police station armed with muffins. They might be day-old muffins, but it's still a potent bribe. "Hey, Cindy!" I place the bag on her desk. "Muffins for Whispering Bay's finest and the world's best receptionist."

Paco looks at me as if to say, *Isn't that laying it on a bit thick?*

He's right, of course, but a little bit of flattery can't hurt the cause.

"Hey, Lucy. Wow. Muffins two days in a row." She eyes the bag. "Did you include some of those low-fat cranberry ones you brought me yesterday?"

"Hel-lo. Of course, I did."

Paco barks to get her attention.

"And hello to you, Paco." She opens a desk drawer to produce a treat. This time Paco doesn't wait to be asked to perform. He immediately sits, then goes down. But he doesn't stop there. He also does a series of rolls, then sits back up and raises his paw in the air.

What a sellout.

"Wow. You've really been working with him. Is it Woofio? Have you been learning his techniques?"

"Nope. He learned those on his own."

She plays with him for a few minutes. "So, what brings you here? If you've come to see Travis, he's not in. Zeke isn't here either." Her voice hitches with pride. "Rusty is in charge right now."

Yes!

With both Travis and Zeke gone, this should be easier. Not a slam-dunk. But my odds of success have just improved dramatically. I make a sad face. "Shoot. I was hoping to surprise Travis. When will he be back?"

"I'm not sure. He left about an hour ago, but he didn't say where he was going."

Unfortunately, that gives me no information. He could be back in five minutes or five hours. I'll have to work fast. "I hear Archie Clements is in custody."

"What a scumbag, huh?" She waves me closer like she wants to tell me more. I'm happy to oblige her. "Do you know he swindled, like, ten people out of money? It's people we know, too. Like Victor Marino and Shirley Dombrowski."

Shirley Dombrowski? I had no idea she was writing a novel, let alone one of Jefferson Pike's victims. Poor Shirley. The thought of her being swindled of what little money she has makes me angry.

"Luckily, Clements is cooperating," says Cindy, "so it looks like everyone will get their money back."

"Well, that's a relief."

"Isn't it?"

"I hear that Clements is going to take the fall for everything and the girl is going to get off scot-free. Do you think he'll get much time?" I ask.

"Probably. But it's not just the charges here he's facing. The FBI is coming to question him for a bunch of other scams."

"The girl, Anita Tremble, she came in The Bistro this morning. She seemed so sweet. It's hard to believe someone like her could get involved with two con men like Archie Clements and Jefferson Pike."

"I thought the same thing," says Cindy. "I brought her some coffee when she was in the interrogation room, and she was just a boo-hooing up a storm. You can't fake tears like hers. Believe me, I've seen plenty of crying at this station, and I can spot a fake a mile away. I hear the DA is going easy on her. I certainly hope she's learned her lesson."

Okay, I think I've set things up nicely. I just hope Cindy buys into my routine.

"You know, Cindy, I'm embarrassed to tell you this, but I was one of the people that Jefferson Pike and Archie Clements targeted for their scheme."

"What? You're kidding! But I thought they were targeting writers. Wait. Lucy, have you written a book? Let me guess. You wrote a cookbook. On muffins."

"I wish." If I could blush on command, I would, but I'm not so shameless as that, so I try my best to seem flustered. "I wrote a romance. A really steamy one."

"Oh. Like *Fifty Shades of Grey* steamy?"

"I wish it was that tame. Mine is a lot steamier."

Cindy giggles. "Lucy McGuffin! What would your—*oh*. That's awkward."

"Tell me about it. I had planned to publish it under a pen name. I gave it to Archie to read. He told me his name was Hoyt Daniels and he was an aspiring author like myself. I know it was foolish of me, but I was just so taken in by them."

She nods. "Like I said, you weren't the only one. How much money did you give them?"

"We never got that far. But, he has my manuscript, Cindy. With my real name on it! What if someone gets ahold of it? What if someone shows it to my brother? I would die of embarrassment."

"Oh, hon. What are you going to do?"

"After I talked to Anita this morning, it gave me hope. If Archie is half the gentleman she says he is, maybe he'll tell me what they did with my manuscript."

"It's worth a try," says Cindy.

"You think so? The thing is, how do I talk to him? If the feds are coming to question him, chances are they'll take him out of state. I'll spend the rest of my life wondering what happened to my book."

"You poor thing. That's awful." She hesitates. "I bet Rusty would let you talk to Archie."

"Really?"

"Why not? If the two of us ask him nicely. Plus, you could always throw in some free muffins for him."

"Just for the rest of his life!" I say.

Cindy smiles coyly. "Let me see what I can do."

I leave Paco with Cindy and follow Rusty down the hallway. He stealthily looks to the right, then to the left, motioning me to follow him. I feel like a ninja on a secret mission. "I hope this isn't going to get you in trouble," I say.

"Nah. I just want to make sure no one's looking."

"I promise, Rusty. Free lemon poppy seed muffins forever."

"Aw, that's okay, Lucy. Cindy told me what happened to you." He clears his throat like he's suddenly uncomfortable, and a wave of tenderness washes over me. Whatever happens, I can't let Rusty or Cindy get in trouble over this.

He ushers me into the interrogation room, where Archie Clements sits at a table, eating one of my carrot cake muffins. He looks up in surprise. "Oh, it's you."

"Well, hello, Hoyt," I say, using his alias.

He shrugs. "Sorry about that little ruse, my dear."

"You have five minutes," warns Rusty. "I'll be watching you from the window. He's not dangerous, but if he makes a move, this visit is over."

"Got it. Thanks."

Rusty points two V-sign fingers between himself and Archie in the universal "I'm watching you" look, then closes the door.

"This is unexpected," says Archie. "But I understand this excellent muffin is compliments of your café. Thank you. The food around here leaves a bit to be desired."

"You're welcome." Because I'm curious, I ask. "Did you select that muffin yourself, or did Cindy just hand it to you?"

"I selected it myself. Very nice variety, by the way."

You know the old saying you can always judge a book by its cover? I have another saying. You can always judge a person by their favorite muffin. Carrot cake muffins are loyal and trustworthy, two qualities I'm having trouble ascribing to Archie Clements right now. Still, it bodes well for our conversation.

He brushes the muffin crumbs from his hands. "What can I do for you, Lucy?"

"Anita Tremble came into my café this morning."

"How is she?"

"Pretty good, considering. She says her lawyer tells her she'll probably get off with just probation. Thanks to you. She says you told the police she was only minimally involved in the scam."

"It's the truth."

"If you say so."

A muscle over his right eye twitches.

I look up at the clock above the door. I have four minutes left. "Anita says that you're a stand-up guy. I'm hoping that's true."

"What do you want?" he asks.

"I don't know if you're aware, but I'm the one who found Jefferson Pike's body. I'd like to ask you a few questions."

He considers this. "It's unusual, but as long as the answers don't incriminate me, I don't see why not."

"Anita told me that Jefferson Pike told you he had a run-in with J.W. Quicksilver."

"That's true."

"But before he let Quicksilver go to the police, he hit him over the head, tied him up and locked him in a closet."

"Yes."

"Did you see this for yourself? Did you see J.W. Quicksilver?"

"I wish I had. Then I could have identified him for the police. Unfortunately, I was too frazzled to think clearly at that point. All I could think of was getting Anita ... was getting away before we were found out."

He can't identify Will! I blow out a slow, deep breath.

"You wanted to leave town right away?"

"Of course, I did. But then, I was always the more prudent one of us. But Jefferson? He liked to live on the edge. He said we had plenty of time to still do the book club sting, collect all the money, and get out of town before Quicksilver was discovered in the closet."

"That must have made you mad."

His eyes flash with anger. "If it wasn't for Jefferson's big ego, he'd still be alive, and I wouldn't be sitting in jail."

It's exactly what Anita said. So far everything Archie has told me has been the truth, but I have to word this next question simply and clearly so that I get a correct readout.

"Did you kill Jefferson Pike?"

"Me? I don't have a violent bone in my body. Besides, what would be my motive?"

"You said yourself you were the prudent one. That made him, what? The reckless one? You could have killed him over any number of things."

"Except I just told you I wanted to leave town quietly to avoid trouble. Killing one's partner has a way of making the police notice you."

"So you didn't kill Jefferson?"

"I already said I didn't."

Archie is telling the truth.

"But if you didn't kill him, who did?"

"Isn't it obvious? It had to be J.W. Quicksilver. He had motive. Jefferson said he was indignant when he confronted him about our scam. And he had opportunity. Sometime before the book club was

scheduled to start, he escaped from his bindings. He must have confronted Jefferson at Betty Jean's house, found him alone and, in a fury,
killed him."

"That's a bit out there, isn't it?"

"It's the only thing that makes sense."

Rusty taps on the window and points to the clock. My time is
almost up.

"Just one more question. I got to Betty Jean's house around five
thirty. That's when I found Jefferson dead. Book club wasn't supposed
to start until seven. What was he doing there so early?"

Archie sits up straight. "Five thirty? That's impossible. Anita and
I got back to the beach house around four that afternoon. Once we
knew we'd been compromised, we packed up and left the beach house
immediately. That was around four fifteen. Jefferson and I argued
because I wanted him to come with us, but he was supposed to meet
with another potential mark at The Harbor House for drinks at five.
He told us to go ahead; he'd meet the mark, then go on to Betty Jean's
house and catch up to us the next day." He frowns. "I didn't realize the
time of death was … You have to be wrong about that. He wouldn't
have missed meeting up with a mark. The game was everything to
Jefferson."

"Maybe the mark didn't show up? Or canceled? And Jefferson
decided to go to Betty Jean's early?"

"Perhaps."

I can tell he's disturbed by what I just told him, but I'm not sure
why or what it means.

"Do you know who this potential mark was?"

"Jefferson didn't give me a name. At that point, I didn't care. I just
wanted Anita and I to get as far away as possible. We would have made
it too, if it wasn't for a faulty taillight."

Rusty taps again on the window, this time more impatiently. I nod, indicating that I'm done.

Archie puts a finger up in the air. "Before you go, may I ask you a question?"

"Sure."

"The night of the book signing at The Harbor House. You said you'd written a romance novel. Was that true?"

I could lie to him, but what would be the point? "No."

He chuckles to himself. "It appears I'm not the only one who gave a good performance that night."

"Guess not."

As productive as this conversation has been, I'm now back to square one, because everything Archie has just told me is the truth.

He isn't the killer.

Chapter Fourteen

I WALK OUT INTO the hallway and run smack into Travis and FBI Agent Patricia Billings.

Uh-oh.

"Well, if it isn't Lucy McGuffin," says Agent Billings. "Funny running into you at police headquarters." It's been a few weeks since I've seen her, so it's too soon to hope that she's changed. She's still starchy. Still steely-eyed. Still too astute. You'd think she'd cut me some slack considering that the last time I saw her I saved her bacon from a mob hit.

"You know me. I brought muffins to the station. Our police work so hard. We have to keep them motivated." I pump my fist in the air for emphasis.

Travis doesn't buy it. "Did you just come out of the interrogation room?"

"What?" I ask, playing innocent. "Is it around here somewhere?"

"Excuse us a moment," he says to Billings. He takes me by the elbow and leads me into Zeke Grant's office, then closes the door shut.

"Should we be in Zeke's office without him?" I ask.

"Don't think for a minute that either Billings or I buy that lost lamb routine of yours. What are you really doing here?"

"Talk about ingrates. Next time I'll bring my muffins to the fire department."

"Lucy."

That one simple word does me in. I can't lie to Travis. I just can't.

"Okay, you got me. I talked to Archie Clements. But don't get mad at Rusty. I totally tricked him into helping me."

Travis looks like he's mentally counting to ten. "You tricked him?" he says in an eerily calm voice. "Why am I not surprised by this? I'd ask what you think you're doing, but I already know. How many times do I have to tell you to leave the police work to the actual police?"

There's a knock on the door. Without waiting for a response, Agent Billings walks inside. "I want to know what you two are talking about. Unless ... " She looks at Travis the way I look at a new muffin recipe I'm thinking of trying out. "Am I interrupting something personal?"

My female instincts kick into high gear. "Yes," I say.

"No," Travis says, at the same time.

"Which one is it?" she asks.

None of your business. "Are you going to take Archie Clements back to Virginia with you?" I ask.

"That's the plan. Why are you interested in Clements?"

"Lucy just spoke to him," says Travis.

Billings snaps to attention. "Really?" She takes the chair behind Zeke's desk and motions for me to sit down as well. "I want to hear all about it."

I cautiously take a seat across from her. "Why should I tell you anything?"

She narrows her eyes at me. "Because I'm a special agent with the FBI and it's your civic duty to aid me in any way I see fit. I'll be honest, in my ten years at the Bureau, I've never met anyone more intuitive than you. Do you know how long my team and I were after El Tigre?" she says, referring to the code name for an assassin sent to kill a mob witness here in Whispering Bay. "In just a few days you were able to sniff out that sociopath. I never asked you how you did it. But I'm asking you now. How did you do it?"

Like I'm really going to tell her that I'm a human lie detector and that my dog is a ghost whisperer. "Just dumb luck, I guess. Plus, Paco helped out." It's the truth. Sort of.

"You mean your dog? I saw him out front with the receptionist. He was rolling around on the ground. I hardly think that chihuahua is a canine Sherlock Holmes."

You'd be surprised.

"What do you want to know?" I ask.

She pulls a file out of her tote and hands it to me. A photo of a younger Archie wearing glasses and dressed in a business suit is stapled to the top of a rap sheet. "Archie Clements and Jefferson Pike ran a real estate swindle on the Eastern seaboard. They were good. Good enough to elude us for years. Archie has never been violent, and now his partner is dead. So what happened here in Whispering Bay to change all that up?"

"You think Archie killed Jefferson?"

"That's what I want you to ask him. I have a feeling that you might be able to tell us if he's lying about that." She stares at me like she can see right through me. It's probably some kind of FBI mind trick, but it works. I'm not the only one in the room who's intuitive. Agent Billings's feelings are right on.

I look at Archie's picture again. Just like his professor disguise, he pulls off the mild-mannered businessman well. "What would be his motive for killing Pike?"

"What's everyone's motive? Money. We figure that over the years, the two of them have hustled at least ten million off their victims."

Ten million dollars. *Holy wow*.

"But that makes no sense. If Jefferson Pike and Archie Clements had ten million dollars stashed away, why come here and pull a small-time publishing scam? What they got here was peanuts compared to ten million."

"Exactly. This sting was unusual for them. For one thing, the potential money to be made was low, and the publishing angle is something they've never done before. They were on their way to Key West and then eventually the Cayman Islands when they stopped here in Whispering Bay. They could have argued about the operation or the money. Or any other number of things."

"I'm still confused. Why do you want my opinion again?"

"Because I want to offer him a deal. A highly reduced sentence in exchange for the location of those ten million dollars. The restitution to his victims will go a long way to softening a federal judge. But he's not getting a cushy deal if he's a murderer."

I hesitate a moment before saying, "As a matter of fact, I already asked him if he killed Jefferson Pike."

She looks at Travis, then back at me. "Did you? I won't ask why you're interested because frankly, I don't care. You can play Nancy Drew all you want, and as long as it benefits me, I'll cheer you on from the sidelines. Jefferson Pike's murder, while messy, is a local matter. The cops here can handle it. Unless, like I said, Archie Clements is the killer. Then that interferes with my case, and it does become my business." She leans forward. "So, what did he say? I want to know your take on it. Did he kill Jefferson Pike?"

"He says he didn't. And I believe him."

She nods crisply. "Good. Frankly, I would have been surprised if he'd done it. Not his style at all."

"So, that's it. You're going to take my word on it?"

"Right now, the evidence doesn't support Archie killing Jefferson Pike," says Travis.

"If the local police aren't going to charge Archie with Jefferson's murder, then that's good enough for me. All that concerns me is clearing this real estate scam off my desk."

"You really think that Archie will tell you where the money is in exchange for a reduced sentence? Because something tells me he's the type that wouldn't mind spending a decade or so in prison if it means coming out to ten million. He's not young, but he's not ancient either."

She pulls another file out of her tote and tosses it across the desk. "Meet Archie Clements's daughter."

I open the file to find a single sheet. At the top is a picture of a young woman with mousy brown hair and frightened-looking eyes. "Anita Tremble is Archie's daughter?"

Boy, did I get that relationship wrong.

"Archie didn't know Anita existed until about six months ago. That's when the mother got in touch with Archie and told him he had a daughter. The girl had been going through a rough patch, and Archie wanted to help her. We're not sure exactly how she got involved in the con, but it's enough to give us the leverage we need against Archie. So far, the charges against her are minimal, but if Archie doesn't cough up the location of that money, then we're prepared to hit Anita with enough charges to keep her in prison for a good five to seven years."

"And you think he cares about her enough to give up the money?"

"I don't know. You tell me."

This one's a no-brainer. "Yes, he's very protective of her. I think he'll tell you where the money is if it helps her."

Billings sits back in the chair, looking satisfied. "Excellent. Your intel is going to help me put the squeeze on this guy." She collects her files and puts them back in her tote. "You know, Lucy, you should think about applying to the Bureau. With your skills, you'd make an excellent interrogator. If you can pass the tests, I'll try to make sure you and Fontaine go through basic training together."

"What?" I flip around in my seat to face Travis. "You're joining the FBI?"

He glares at Agent Billings before saying, "I'm thinking about it."

"Oh. I thought ... Never mind." It makes sense now. Travis and Patricia Billings aren't *involved*. She's recruiting him for the FBI.

If Travis joins the FBI, then that means he'll be leaving Whispering Bay. Which means he can't seriously want to date me. Which means I'm off the hook. I don't have to worry about hurting his feelings when I tell him that I've chosen Will. This is great news.

Only, for some reason, it doesn't feel great. My chest feels tight. I think I know how the Grinch felt when his heart suddenly grew three sizes too big. Except my heart was already regular size, so this doesn't feel good at all.

I can't believe it, but I think I'm going to miss the big lug.

"Don't think too long about that offer," Agent Billings says to him. "Opportunities like this don't come around often." She puts her tote over her shoulder. "Thanks again, Lucy. Looks like I owe you twice now." She walks out the door and calls for Rusty to take her to see Archie Clements.

"The FBI, huh?" I say to Travis.

"Sorry, I didn't want you to find out like that. I told her I was thinking about it. Doesn't mean I'm going to take it."

"Well, you should. It sounds like a great opportunity. You don't want to be stuck here in Whispering Bay for the rest of your life, do you?"

He goes to say something, then shakes his head instead. But it feels like it might have been the most important thing that anyone's ever said to me.

"What were you going to say?" I hold my breath waiting for his answer.

"I was going to say how lucky you are that your little scheme to visit Archie Clements didn't blow up in your face."

That's not what he was going to say, but I'll give him a pass.

"If I ask you a question, will you tell me the truth?" he asks.

"It depends on the question."

He raises a brow at me.

"Hey, I'm being honest here."

"I'm going to go one step further than Billings. In your truth or dare session with Clements, did you ask him who did kill Jefferson Pike?"

Oh no. I swallow hard. "Yes."

"And what did he say?"

"He doesn't know who killed him. He wasn't there, so it's not like he's a witness or anything."

"But he has an idea?"

"Yes," I squeak.

"And?" he prompts impatiently.

Once again, I'm faced with a conundrum. I could lie to Travis. I could tell him anything and he wouldn't know if I was telling the truth or not, but something here isn't right. My stomach curls into a knot. Just like before, I can't lie to him. It's ... *physically* impossible. *What's going on here*?

"Archie thinks that the real J.W. Quicksilver is the killer. But that doesn't mean he's right. It's just what he thinks. Which means it could be anyone. How many people did they swindle in Whispering Bay? Ten? And that's just here. What about all those other people they swindled in all those other scams? It sounds to me like there's a lot of people who had a motive to kill Pike."

"True. That's why I'm not ruling anyone out. At this point in the investigation, all of Pike's victims, including J.W. Quicksilver, are suspect, and I'm bringing them all in for questioning."

"But you don't know J.W. Quicksilver's real identity, so how are you going to find him to bring him in?"

"I don't know his identity yet. But I will. And soon."

"How? He's like the world's most reclusive author."

"Simple. I called his publisher in New York and explained the situation. I told them I needed J.W. Quicksilver's real name and address in connection with a murder investigation."

"And they just gave it to you?"

"No, but I got a friendly judge involved, and he issued an order at noon today. Quicksilver's publishing company has twenty-four hours to cough up his name or be held in contempt of court." He grins. "I figure if J.W. Quicksilver is still in the area, I'll have him in my jail for questioning by lunchtime tomorrow."

Chapter Fifteen

"THIS IS BAD," I tell Will. In the past fifteen minutes, I've managed to nearly pace a hole in his living-room rug, with Paco following in my tracks. "Really bad."

Will, who up to now has been listening silently while I've filled him in on what's happening down at the police station, pushes his glasses up his nose. "Then there's nothing left to do but go to the police."

"What did your editor say when he called?"

When I got to Will's house, he was on a conference call with both his editor and his agent. "He said it was my decision if I wanted to come out. That the publishing house would be happy to fight the court order."

I stop pacing. "They're going to go to bat for you? That's awesome."

"It's not as noble as you think. My agent is nearly giddy at the thought of all the publicity this is going to create."

"Publicity? I don't get it."

"What do you think is going to happen when the publishing house refuses to give the cops my identity? Word will get out in the press that the reclusive J.W. Quicksilver is connected to a publishing scam and a murder. It'll be all over social media in five minutes. I'll go viral for a couple of days, my book sales will skyrocket, and everyone will make a nice fat profit. Then a week later when the buzz dies, the publishing company will give their lawyers the go-ahead to stop fighting the court order. They'll give me up, and two months from now when someone Googles my name, the first thing they'll see is that I was a suspect in a murder investigation. Sales will still be good, but my name—my real name—will be mud forever."

I sit down, stunned. "But you're *innocent*."

"No one will care about that, Lucy. All anyone sees is the headlines. The click bait. The real story will be buried at the bottom of the page. No one bothers to read to the end anymore."

A blast of anger shoots through me. "We're not going to let that happen."

"How are we going to stop it?"

"Travis says the publishing company has until twelve tomorrow to give up your name. All we have to do is find the killer in the next ... " I look at my watch. "Nineteen hours and forty-three minutes."

"Oh, sure. That gives us plenty of time."

"Don't be such a negative Nelly. Didn't you ever pull an all-nighter in college? Besides, you're forgetting. You have a secret weapon. Me. I'm on your side."

Paco barks as if to say, *Me too*!

Will shakes his head, then chuckles wearily. "Okay, Lucy. I know better than to try to fight you on this. Where do we start?"

The three of us get in my car and head over to Victor Marino's house. Since he's one of the two victims whose identities I'm aware of, it's the logical place to begin. Plus, Victor knows I know he's been scammed, so we can cut right to the chase.

Victor lives in a quiet neighborhood, just a few blocks from Betty Jean's. He answers the door on the first ring, takes one look at us, and ushers us inside. "I'm honored. Come in, come in!" He practically trips over himself in his glee.

If I thought for one moment all this was for me, I'd be flattered. But I know exactly which of the three of us Victor is so giddy to see. And it's not Will either.

"I never thought I'd have the honor of hosting Cornelius in my home. Please, take a seat anywhere," he says to Paco.

Paco looks at his choices. A nice little leather sofa or two recliners. He hops up on the sofa, circles around four times, then hunkers down with a grin on his face. I sit next to my dog, and Will takes one of the recliners.

"His name is Paco now, remember?" I say to Victor.

He nods eagerly. "Whatever you say. Do you think he's thirsty? Is he hungry? I have steak."

At the word "steak," Paco's ears perk up.

"I don't give Paco steak. Or any other human food either. The vet says it's bad for him." This is a lie because I give Paco human food all the time. Just not steak.

Victor looks horrified. "I would never do anything to endanger this sweet little dog." He sits on the other side of Paco. "Am I permitted to pet him? Or will it interfere with his aura?"

Oh, for the love of ... "Yes, you can pet him. But we're not here because of anything ghost-related. We need your help with something. It's about the Jefferson Pike murder."

"That man," he seethes. "The way he strutted into town pretending to be J.W. Quicksilver, swindling poor, innocent people out of their hard-earned money. And it wasn't just the money. He gave them false hope. He made us all believe we'd be published by a fancy company. The man should be shot."

"Actually, he was stabbed."

Victor reddens. "Yes, of course, he was. And now I hear that the real J.W. Quicksilver is here in town and that he's the prime suspect. Who would have thought? It's like something out of one of his novels."

"That's fake news," I say. "J.W. Quicksilver is most certainly not the murderer, and we need your help to clear his name. You're a big fan of his. Don't you want to help him out?"

"Yes, of course I do." Victor's eyes widen. "Lucy, are you telling me that you've been in contact with the real J.W.? What's he like? Do you think he'd be interested in reading my novel?"

Will and I exchange glances. "Lucy isn't at liberty to reveal Quicksilver's identity," says Will. "Right now, the man is fighting for his life and his reputation."

Victor collects himself. "Of course. But what can I do to help?"

"You can give us the names of the other scam victims," I say.

"How would I know their names?"

"Because Archie Clements offered me a deal. If I gave him the names of other aspiring authors who might be interested in their publishing venture, then I wouldn't have to give them as much money to get in. I'm assuming he offered that little discount to everyone."

Victor looks taken aback. "Lucy, you wrote a book too?"

"No, I just pretended. It was a trick." At the perplexed look on his face, I wave my hand in the air. "It's a long story. So, what's it going to be? Are you going to help J.W. Quicksilver or not?"

He mulls this over a bit, then glances down at Paco, who's looking up at him like he's waiting for the answer as well. "What's in it for me?" Victor asks finally.

This was not the answer I was expecting. Victor has always been so sweet. So …

Oh no. I don't like the way he's looking at Paco.

"What's in it for you is the good feeling you'll get when you help bring the real killer to justice."

"Why don't you get the names from the police?" Before I can answer, he says, "I'll tell you why. Because they won't give it to you, will they? No, they won't. Travis Fontaine wants to solve this murder on his own." He continues petting Paco. "I'm not saying that I have the names. And I'm not saying that I don't. But let's say that I did have the names. The people on that list aren't going to be happy that I gave them up. Not if you're going to go around snooping in their business and accusing them of murder."

"How about we get right down to it? What do you want?"

"You know what I want. It's what I've always wanted. The chance to see Cornelius in action."

Paco wags his tail.

"You see?" Victor says stubbornly. "He wants it too."

Will catches my eye again. This time he points to his watch. I know. I know. We're running out of time. Ack. I can't believe I'm going to do this.

"Okay, you win. I'll let you and the Sunshine Ghost Society have Paco for one séance."

Victor claps his hands in glee. "Oh, Lucy! Thank you!"

"But," I add sternly, "it has to be under the conditions I lay down. I'll want a veterinary professional to be present to monitor the whole thing. Paco can't be hurt or compromised in any way."

"Of course, of course. Whatever you say!" He gets up from the couch. "I'll go find a pen and paper and make out that list. Wait till Phoebe and the rest of the society hear of this," he chortles.

"I can't believe I just sold out my own dog in exchange for this ... list," I say in disgust on the way back to my car.

Victor's list only had four names, including himself. Which was kind of tricky if you ask me. We've just visited the last person on the list. All of whom turned out to be a huge bust. Including Phoebe Van Cleave, who's writing a book about a female ghost detective who lives in a small Florida town. Will and I were forced to listen to the synopsis for her story before she'd answer any of our questions.

"Is everyone in this town writing a thinly veiled novel about themselves?" I ask.

"Looks like it." Will leans back in the car seat and closes his eyes. "So, what do we do now?"

"There have to be more victims. I just don't know how to find out who they are."

He nods in resignation. Poor Will. He could lose everything he's worked so hard for all these years. Any residual anger I had about his not telling me he was J.W. Quicksilver flew out the window a long time ago.

The air in the car reeks of gloom and doom. I wish I could make him laugh.

"We could always storm police headquarters, hold Rusty hostage, and demand Travis tell us the names of the other victims. And if he still refuses, we can sic Paco on him."

Will smiles while still keeping his eyes closed. "Sounds like a plan."

"Did you know that Travis is thinking about working for the FBI?" I blurt.

His eyes pop open. "Where did you hear that?"

"Agent Billings. She's encouraging him to apply."

He shrugs. "Fontaine is a good cop. And smart. He'd probably do okay at the Bureau."

It's the first time I've heard Will compliment Travis in a long time. "The night of the reading, after Travis found us in the storage room. What did you and he talk about?"

Will shifts uncomfortably in his seat. "Guy stuff."

"Guy stuff that included me?"

"Maybe."

"If you talked about me, then shouldn't I know what you said?"

As if to emphasize my point, Paco pushes his head from the back seat to nudge Will's elbow. My dog is the best wingman ever.

"Well?" I demand.

"I asked him what his intentions were. Regarding you."

"I'm twenty-six years old. I don't need anyone to ask a man what his intentions are."

"I know that," he says uncomfortably.

"Who do you think you are?" I joke. "My big brother?"

He turns and looks at me.

Holy wow. Brittany was spot on.

All these years I thought I was in love with Will. And maybe I was, in a teenage girl kind of way, but I don't get the same tingly kind of feeling when I'm around him that I get with …

I groan.

"This thing between us. It isn't going to work."

"I know," he says quietly. "I love you, Lucy. You're my best friend. When I saw that Fontaine was interested in you, I think I got scared. Sebastian and I were best buds for all those years, and when he chose the priesthood, well, I was happy for him. It's his calling. But it always comes first. As it should. When I think of my life without you in it—"

"Why would you ever not be in my life? What? Because I might have a boyfriend?" I laugh-snort. "What do you take me for? One of those girls who put bros before hoes?"

Will laughs. "What?"

"Oh, just ask Betty Jean. She knows what it means. The thing is, I love you too. And you'll always be in my life. Even if we're both married to other people and have eight kids apiece, you'll always be my best friend."

"Lucy, I am not having eight kids."

"Well, neither am I. It was just an expression."

"Now that we've cleared that up," he says, "I want to say something."

Uh-oh. This sounds serious.

"I didn't tell you that I was J.W. Quicksilver because ... it's not because I didn't trust you or that I didn't want you to know. The only reason Sebastian found out was because I wanted to donate the money to pay for the new roof for St. Perpetua's, and he insisted on knowing where the money came from. It's just that the stuff I write, it comes from a place inside me that I'm not even aware of sometimes. Being anonymous makes it easy for me to not hold back. If everyone knows that Will Cunningham is the author, I'm afraid I'll be too safe with my choices."

I take it all in. "Yeah, I get it."

"Does this mean you're not mad at me anymore?"

I roll my eyes. "Come here." I reach out and hug him, and for the first time, it feels ... *right*. He still smells heavenly, like a fine old leather-bound book encased in the slightest hint of cologne. But he's just Will. My best friend. My big brother. My cohort in crime (so to speak).

My phone goes off. We break away to glance at the screen. It's Betty Jean. "What's Betty Jean doing calling you at nine o'clock at night?" he asks.

"Oh no." I put her on speakerphone. "Hey, Betty Jean, I'm so sorry."

"You should be. Dinner is getting cold. When you will be here?"

"Um. Five minutes? And could you put an extra plate on the table? Will's going to join us."

She makes a growling sound. "With pleasure."

Chapter Sixteen

"That's the best beef stew I've ever tasted," says Will. "Thank you." He pats his tummy appreciatively, then smiles across the table at Betty Jean, who openly leers at him because some things never change.

"Glad you liked it," she says. Thank goodness she's ditched the Farrah Fawcett wig and the Spanx. Her hair is back to normal, and without all the mascara she'd been caking on in the past few days, her blue eyes seem clearer. I've never noticed before because her big personality overshadows it, but she's an attractive woman. I bet when she was younger, she was a real knockout. No wonder she was able to, as she puts it, "snare" four husbands.

Will offers to do the dishes, and I'm more than happy to let him. He goes back and forth between my kitchen and the dining room, clearing plates and cleaning up.

"Yes, thanks for dinner," I say. "And sorry again for being so late."

"Just where were you kids anyway?" she asks.

Why not tell her? It's not exactly a secret. "Trying to figure out who killed Jefferson Pike."

"Any luck?"

"Not really. Pretty much everyone who had a motive to dislike the man has an alibi for the time of his murder."

"I hear the real J.W. Quicksilver is the prime suspect. I hear he came to town and confronted Jefferson Pike and the two of them had a big fight and that he killed him. Which means the real J.W. Quicksilver was in my house." Her eyes go round. "Looks like I got J.W. Quicksilver to my book club meeting after all. Just a couple of hours too early. Too bad no one knows his real name or what he looks like. He might be a murderer, but to the people in this town that Jefferson Pike swindled, he's a hero."

"Where on earth did you hear all that?" I ask.

"Table number six. I had no idea how much gossip you could pick up working here. You must know everything juicy that happens in this town."

Will rejoins us in the dining room. "Lucy tells me that you helped at the café today. That was nice of you."

"Oh yeah. Easy peasy. I'll have to get some better shoes, but I think I can make it work."

"Make what work?" I ask.

"Sarah asked if I could stay on a few mornings a week, so I said, sure, why not?" She winks at Will. "That way I'll get first crack at all the best gossip."

"She mentioned something about that," I say carefully. "But we haven't fully discussed it yet."

"Well she went ahead and hired me. On account of how you're going to be busy once she goes into business with that Heidi Burrows."

I go still. "*What*?"

"And I thought I needed a hearing aid," Betty Jean mutters. "For partners, the two of you sure do seem out of whack. That's why she left early today. To go over to Heidi's Bakery."

"Lucy," Will warns, seeing the expression on my face, "don't jump to any conclusions. I'm sure there's a logical explanation behind that."

There's a logical explanation, all right. Sarah wants to ditch our partnership. Not that I blame her. Ever since I've found my first dead body, disaster has become my middle name. I'm always running out the door on some emergency or other, leaving her stuck to do her job and mine. No wonder she's looked so tired lately.

How long have she and Heidi been planning this? Long enough to be quoting the same marketing tactics, that's how long.

The only thing that doesn't make sense is her offer to cover Will's loan. Except ... it does make sense. Sarah is the nicest person I know. If she's planning to leave me, then she's probably feeling horribly guilty. Paying off Will's loan is her way of making it up to me.

I feel worse than I did last Christmas morning when I ate the entire bag of dark-chocolate-covered almonds.

"You look sick," says Betty Jean. "I hope it wasn't my beef stew."

I shake off my feeling of despondency. "No, it's this ... murder case."

"So is it true? Did Quicksilver murder Pike?"

"No," I say firmly. "And please, if you hear any more rumors claiming that he did, I'd appreciate it if you'd nip those in the bud fast."

"Sounds like this is personal," she says.

"I just don't like to see an innocent person railroaded for a crime they didn't commit."

"If J.W. didn't kill Pike, who did?"

"Like I said, that's what Will and I have been trying to figure out."

"Maybe I can help," she says. "Most likely I was the last person to see him alive. Besides the killer."

Good idea. Why didn't I think to ask Betty Jean before? Probably because I wasn't sure she'd be honest with me. Considering what I think happened between her and Jefferson Pike.

"Are you sure you want to answer our questions?" I ask cautiously.

"Sure, go ahead."

Okay, here goes.

"The book club meeting was scheduled for seven, but you said Jefferson Pike got there early to help set up. What time was that?"

"Around four thirty."

Archie claims he and Anita left town at four fifteen. Which means after they left the beach house, Jefferson must have come straight over to Betty Jean's.

"Archie Clements told me that Jefferson was scheduled to meet a potential mark at The Harbor House at five for drinks before coming over to the book club meeting. Obviously, he never made it. Do you know why?"

Betty Jean makes an oops face. "Because I was the person he was supposed to meet for drinks but I invited him to come over early to my place instead."

"You're writing a book too?" Will asks.

"Nah. I just said that to get his attention."

Will fights back a smirk. That's just so Betty Jean.

"Did Pike know that you had no intention of buying into his scheme?" I ask.

"He did once he got to my place."

I can't keep beating around the bush and keeping a straight face at the same time, so I'll just come out with it. "Did the two of you sleep together?"

"No. But we did have sex. No sleeping involved." She clicks her tongue in disappointment. "I thought after all those hot sex scenes he wrote in his books, he'd be a little bit more entertaining in the sack, but he was just your typical sixty-five-year-old."

I don't even want to know what that means.

I glance over to gauge Will's reaction. His face is redder than a cherry.

"So, after the two of you, uh—"

"Knocked boots? I told him I needed to go to the grocery store to get more wine for the book club meeting. But that was just an excuse to get out of the house. We had a whole hour and half before the group showed up, and I wasn't about to sit there and make small talk, you know?"

"But you did go to the Piggly Wiggly, right?"

"Oh, sure. I got an extra bottle of wine, just in case. I was going to drive around the block to kill some time until six, because that's when I was expecting you to show up, but then I saw the police cars coming to my house."

"Let me get this straight. Jefferson Pike came to your house around four thirty-ish. You left at five to go to the Piggly Wiggly. And since you were expecting me, you left me a note telling me the door was open."

She blanches. "I practically invited the killer to come inside."

"It's not your fault, Betty Jean," says Will.

I continue. "So someone came to your house sometime between five and five thirty, walked inside, found Jefferson sitting on the chair, maybe asleep, even, then got a knife from your kitchen drawer and stabbed him. They wiped the knife clean and left it on the coffee table and walked out the door again."

"Pretty cold, huh?" she says.

"During the time Jefferson and you were together," I say, "did you hear anyone come to the door? Or did your phone ring? Any strange sounds?"

She raises a brow.

Let me rephrase that.

"Any strange sounds coming from *outside* the bedroom?"

"Nope. Nothing. Of course, I did have the music kind of loud, so it's possible the phone might have rung and we wouldn't have heard it. We were kind of busy, you know?"

Just out of curiosity, I ask, "What music did you have on?"

"'Let's Get It On' by Marvin Gaye."

Figures. I clear my throat. "And that's it. You can't remember anything else?"

"Nope. I wish I could be more help. Maybe one of my pervert neighbors saw something."

Will looks at me and frowns.

"What's that supposed to mean?" I ask.

"One of my neighbors is a peeping Tomasina. Either that or a peeping Tom in drag." She gets up from the table, goes into the guest room and comes back out with an earring, then lays it on the table in front of us. It's the earring I found on the grass outside her window the night of Pike's murder.

"That's not mine," she says.

I almost say I know, but I bite my tongue. "What has that to do with anything?"

"You said you found this underneath the second window on the side of the house, near the hibiscus bushes, right?"

"Yes, that's right."

"That window belongs to my bedroom. Someone, wearing this earring, has been spying on me. Maybe even that night. Whoever it was, I hope they got their kicks."

"Do you have any idea who it might be?" I ask.

"Someone who likes sparkly things?" she says dryly.

Considering that Betty Jean was decked out recently a la Farrah Fawcett, she doesn't have room to be critical.

I pick up the earring and inspect it once more. She has a point. It's a rhinestone. And it is sparkly ...

My heart starts to pound.

I realize now that this earring looks familiar. It looks exactly like the earrings Shirley Dombrowski had on the day I went by the rectory to see Sebastian, shortly before I discovered Jefferson Pike's dead body.

Chapter Seventeen

"Shirley Dombrowski? Sebastian's secretary? *That* Shirley? Lucy, are you insane?" asks Will. "She's like the sweetest lady in the world. I have no idea what we're doing here."

Paco, who refused to let us leave the house without him, looks up at me like he's in agreement. The three of us are at Shirley's front door, waiting for her to answer the ringer.

"Even the sweetest lady in the world can be a little kinky. You should have seen her reaction when Jefferson Pike came out on that stage doing his Sean Connery imitation. She was like a giddy schoolgirl." I ring the doorbell again.

"That doesn't mean she's a voyeur."

"Maybe not. But that's her earring I found outside of Betty Jean's window, and I want to know how it got there. We have thirteen hours left to figure out who killed Jefferson Pike, and I don't intend to rest until we do."

The porch lights come on and the door opens a crack. "Yes?" Shirley blinks in surprise. "Oh, Lucy, dear. It's you. And Paco. And Will

Cunningham?" She opens the door wide and ushers us into her living room. She's wearing a robe, and her hair is in curlers. A crucifix hangs above the fireplace mantel.

"What are you all doing here? It's almost eleven o'clock." Her face pales. "Oh no. Don't tell me something has happened to Father. Is Sebastian all right?" She pulls a set of rosary beads from the pocket of her robe and makes a sign of the cross.

Will gives me an *I told you so* look. "Sebastian is fine," he says. "And we're sorry to disturb you so late. Believe me, this wasn't my idea."

I cringe. Standing here seeing Shirley look so ... Shirley-ish, I have to admit I might have overreacted. But like I told Will, I'm determined to find out what happened. "I'm sorry we alarmed you, but it's important we talk to you tonight."

"Shall I make tea?" she asks, clearly still confused over our presence.

"Thank you, but that's not necessary. We just have a few questions, and then we'll leave." I pull the earring from my purse and hand it to her. "I think this is yours."

She recognizes it and chuckles. "It's my earring! Where did you find it? I've been looking for it ever since ... " She stops cold. "Oh dear."

"I found it the night Jefferson Pike was murdered. Right outside Betty Jean's bedroom window. Do you want to tell us what you were doing there?"

She covers her face with her hands. "I'm so ashamed. Please don't tell Father McGuffin. I don't think I could ever look him in the eye again if he knew what I did."

Oh boy. This doesn't sound good at all. Surely, the court will go easy on her, what with her age and the fact that she probably has a spotless record.

"It's okay, Shirley. Just tell us what happened," I urge gently.

"That day, after you came by the rectory, I tried to finish my work, but I was just so excited about the book club meeting and the chance to speak to J.W.—well, he wasn't J.W. Quicksilver, was he? I was so excited, I wasn't thinking rationally. I left early, around four thirty, instead of my usual five. To see if Betty Jean needed any help with the refreshments," she adds, wringing her hands together.

"What happened then?"

"I got to her house and rang the doorbell, but no one answered."

"So you went around to the back?"

"Her car was in the driveway, and there was this awful music blaring, so I knew she had to be inside. I knocked on the back door too, but there was still no answer, so I became terribly worried."

"Worried enough that you tried to peek through the windows?"

Shirley catches the skepticism in my tone. "Young lady, when a woman gets to be a certain age and she lives alone, she appreciates anyone who cares enough to snoop inside and make sure that she's all right."

My cheeks go warm. I've just been deservedly chastised by the secretary of St. Perpetua's Catholic Church. "I'm sorry. You're right, of course."

"Imagine my shock when I saw Betty Jean was ... "

"Discovering what was beneath Jefferson Pike's kilt?"

"*Exactly*. Once I was satisfied that Betty Jean wasn't lying on the floor with a broken hip, I immediately left her house. After that, I had no intention of returning for the book club meeting. I didn't find out about the murder until the next morning."

"And that's it?"

"What else is there?"

Huh. Everything Shirley has said tonight is true. Not that I ever really thought she was capable of murder. But ... well, you never know.

"When you were at the house, making sure that Betty Jean was all right, did you see or hear anything unusual?"

"Just that horrible music."

"I heard that you were one of the people that Jefferson Pike and Archie Clements swindled in their publishing scam. Is that true?"

Poor Shirley. She looks mortified. "Yes, I was one of their foolish victims. But I'm getting all my money back. Rusty and Travis told me once the FBI clears the investigation, I should get a check. It might not be a lot of money to most people, but five thousand dollars for me ... well, you probably know because of your brother, but my late husband didn't leave me in a very good position."

"I'm glad you're getting your money back, Shirley." And then because I can't help myself, I say, "So you wrote a novel?"

Her face lights up. "Oh, I've written a dozen. Thank you for asking! I have the copies in my den. Wait, let me show you." She hops from her chair and scurries into the next room. That's one impressive hip replacement.

Will leans over and whispers, "Now look what you've done."

"Quiet!" I hiss seconds before Shirley comes back carrying a huge manila folder in her hand.

"No one's read them. Except that Jefferson Pike when he was pretending to be J.W. Quicksilver. He said they were wonderful. But of course, that was because he was trying to get my five thousand dollars." She frowns. "Do you think he just pretended to read them?" She shakes her head. "Anyway, I know you don't read these kinds of books," she says to Will, "but everyone in town knows you have excellent literary tastes. Would you mind reading them and giving me your opinion?"

Will gives me a look, then takes the envelope from her hand and opens it up. I lean over to see to a dozen neat little paperclipped packets inside. Will pulls one out. "*The Case of the Perplexed Parishioner*," he reads aloud. "That's the title of your story?"

She nods enthusiastically. "That's the first one. They all center around a widow who works as the secretary at a Catholic church in north Florida. She solves murder mysteries."

"Sounds fascinating," Will chokes out.

I give him a pleading look. "Will would love to read your stories," I say.

"You would?" Shirley asks him eagerly.

Will doesn't miss a beat. "It would be an honor."

And *this* is just one of the many reasons why he'll always be my best friend.

He stands. "I think we've taken up enough of your time, Shirley. Thanks."

"When do you think you can get back to me?" she asks. "With your critique?"

"Um, give me a couple of weeks," he says.

We're almost to the door when I remember something. "Shirley, I'm confused. You said you were ashamed about something. Something that you didn't want Sebastian to find out or you could never look him in the eye again. What were you talking about?"

"Why, leaving the rectory thirty minutes before I was supposed to, of course. What did you think I was talking about?"

Will waits until we're in the car to bust out laughing.

I slink down in my seat. "Okay, so I was wrong about Shirley."

Even Paco looks like he's laughing. I can see all of his teeth. "Did you eat an onion today?" I ask my dog. "Because your breath is out of control." He clamps his jaws shut. "You did, didn't you?" He lifts his chin in the air like he's not going to dignify my question.

"I could have told you that Shirley didn't kill Jefferson Pike," says Will. "No special skills needed there. Admit it, Lucy. This is a dead end. We aren't going to figure this out in the next twelve hours, so we might as well get some sleep."

As much as I hate to agree, Will is right.

"There's no need to get my publishing company involved. First thing tomorrow morning, I'll go down to the police station and tell Fontaine that I'm J.W. Quicksilver."

Chapter Eighteen

I HAVE TROUBLE SLEEPING, but I force myself to stay in bed until four, then I get up, take Paco for a walk and start to make the muffins. Betty Jean comes down into the kitchen around four thirty wearing another one of my favorite T-shirts. The slogan reads MUFFINS RULE, DOUGHNUTS DROOL.

I point to the shirt. "I hope you don't stretch that out."

"Now that's a proper morning greeting," she says chirpily. "Nothing like waking up to a good side of snark to go with your coffee."

"You don't have to be up so early," I say.

"I haven't slept past five since I was seventy." She takes a sip of her coffee. "Did you figure out who killed Jefferson Pike?"

I put a batch of pumpkin chocolate chip muffins in the oven and set the timer. "No."

"Don't look so glum. You can't win 'em all, kid. That makes you, what? Three for four now?" she says, referring to my track record for catching murderers.

"I guess so." Except this time, I've let Will down. In just a few hours, the world will know that he's J.W. Quicksilver, and his name will be forever linked with a murder investigation.

I need to make more muffins. Baking for me releases endorphins the way running does for other people. Plus, since I missed my regular baking session yesterday morning, we could use the extra batches to catch up on inventory.

I'm on my third batch of my famous apple walnut cream cheese muffins when Jill and Sarah walk through the door at the same time. "Yum! Someone's been baking up a storm," says Sarah, who appears well rested today. She surveys the countertops. "Looks like you've been super productive this morning."

"Just practicing for the day I'll have to do it all on my own," I snap.

Yikes. That sounded a bit aggressive.

Jill and Betty Jean give each other a look. Paco looks at me as if to say, *Someone hasn't had their coffee yet*.

"I'll go check out the pantry supplies," says Jill.

Betty Jean follows her lead. "And I'll go wipe down the tables. Again."

They scurry off, leaving Sarah and I alone in the kitchen. Paco looks at the door like he's thinking about bolting too but then changes his mind and lies back down in his corner.

"Sorry, I shouldn't have snapped at you," I say to Sarah. "I didn't get much sleep last night."

"That's all right," Sarah says kindly. "I know this Jefferson Pike murder has you busy."

"Only it shouldn't. I'm a baker. I own half a café. At least, for now I do. I shouldn't be running around playing amateur detective. Travis is right. I need to leave the police work to the professionals."

"But you're so good at it. If it wasn't for you, the mob might have taken over Whispering Bay."

She has a point. But what good are my detective skills if I lose the one thing I've dreamed of all my life? Running my own café. I can't do it without a partner. I don't have the resources.

If anything, living with Betty Jean these past couple of days has taught me to say what I think. "What good is solving crime if I lose my business? Or my partner?"

"What are you talking about?"

"I know what's going on. I know you want to go into business with Heidi. It's okay. I don't blame you. Just … tell me how we're going to do this, so I'll know what to expect."

"You think I want to go into business with Heidi Burrows?" Sarah sounds truly shocked.

"Don't you?"

"No! At least, not like you think." She sits on a stool and chuckles.

"I'm glad you think this is funny."

She tries to look serious. "Sorry, but the idea of leaving you and going into business with that pretentious Heidi is just … well, it's ridiculous."

"I'm confused. If you're not going into business with Heidi, what are the two of you doing playing kitchen together? And you hired Betty Jean without consulting me. When you offered to loan me the money to pay Will back, I thought it was just you being nice, but now I think it's because you feel guilty on account of—wait. You think Heidi is pretentious?" I sag against the kitchen counter. "Thank goodness. I thought I was the only one."

"Half the town thinks that. But she is a good baker. And she makes an excellent donut."

"Because it's laden with a mountain of fat," I mutter.

"Exactly. Heidi came to me a week ago and asked if I'd consider helping her figure out a way to reduce the fat content in her doughnuts. She wants to offer her customers low-fat options. But I'm not the baker here. You are. I told her I couldn't help her, and you're way too busy in our kitchen to help her in hers, so I did a little market research and came up with another idea." She hops down from the stool, pulls out her work bag and hands me a sheet of paper.

"What's this?"

"It's an idea I came up with in one of my marketing classes." Sarah flushes. "I didn't want to tell anyone until I'd finished my first semester. Except Luke. He knows, of course. But I've gone back to school part-time to get my business degree."

"Sarah! That's great!"

"It's all online nowadays so it's super convenient, but I am burning the candle at both ends. That's why I hired Betty Jean, because we need the help. But you're right, I should have okay'd it with you first."

I read through Sarah's marketing plan. Then I read it again for good measure. "You want me to supply muffins for Heidi's bakery?"

"And the Piggly Wiggly. If you think you have time. Let's face it, Lucy. You make the world's best muffins. Why shouldn't the rest of the planet get in on it?"

Sarah leans over my shoulder and points to a column on the page. "We can market them as Lucy's World-Famous Muffins. It's a win-win for everyone. Heidi can offer her customers some lower fat options, and we can use the local grocery store for market testing to see if we want to sell your muffins on a larger scale one day. But for now, if my numbers are right, just selling to Heidi and the Piggly Wiggly will increase our profit margin. You can pay Will off faster. Or me. If you decide to take me up on the loan offer."

I'm stunned. "And Heidi has agreed to sell my muffins in her bakery?"

"She's not dumb, Lucy. She knows it'll be good for her business. Look, hiring Betty Jean gives you more time in the kitchen doing what you do best. Baking. And it gives me some time off to study. But if you don't want her around, I'll make something up and let her go. We can find someone else."

"Find someone else? Just when I'm getting used to her?"

Sarah laughs. "I hate to say this, but you're actually beginning to sound just like her."

"Bite your tongue." Boy, have I gotten everything wrong lately. First, there was the Jefferson Pike investigation. I was so certain that Archie must have killed his partner. Then there was the thing with Shirley. And now Sarah. I think my Spidey sense needs an oil change. "So we're good? Still partners?"

"Always."

"In that case, I'm okay keeping the loan the way it is. Will doesn't mind, and I don't either anymore." I playfully cringe. "And, do you mind if I leave a couple of hours early today? I promised Will I'd meet him for something really important. I'll be back by two to do final cleanup. As a matter of fact, I'll show Betty Jean how to do it."

Sarah, who hates final cleanup more than anything, grins. "You're on."

At quarter to noon, I hang up my apron and grab my car keys. Betty Jean is in the kitchen, chopping apples. "Do you mind covering the counter? I need to do something. I already ran it past Sarah."

"Jeez. What did you people do without me? Sure, go on." She puts down the knife and waves me off.

"Thanks. When I get back, I'll go through the final cleanup with you."

"Oh goody. I can hardly wait."

I chuckle to myself, then head outside into the bright sunlight. It's a gorgeous December day, but suddenly my stomach is curled in knots. Poor Will. What's going to happen to him?

I click on Paco's leash. "C'mon, boy. We're going to visit Cindy." He happily jumps in the car.

When we arrive at the police station, the parking lot is full. Five dark-colored sedans take up the first row. "Those are FBI cars," I say to Paco. "What are they still doing here?"

I spot Will's car in the next row. My heart is beating so fast, it feels like it's going to burst from my chest. I head into the station. Cindy looks up at me, but she doesn't smile. "Lucy," she says in a low voice. "Now isn't a good time." Paco starts to go through his trick routine, but she barely looks at him. He sits up, dejected.

"What's going on? Where's Will?"

"Will Cunningham?" She shrugs. "I think he came to see Travis."

"Why is the FBI still here? I thought they took Archie Clements yesterday and left."

"That was the plan. Not that the FBI tells me anything, mind you, but after you left last night all heck broke loose."

When I left the police station yesterday, Agent Billings was going to try to cut a deal with Archie Clements. A lighter sentence in exchange for his giving up the money. Billings had leverage too, in the form of Anita Tremble. The whole thing seemed pretty cut-and-dried, but obviously if the feds are still here, something must have gone wrong.

"I'll just wait here. If you don't mind?"

"Suit yourself," says Cindy. "But you're going to have a long wait."

I find a chair and a magazine. The next hour goes by excruciatingly slowly. Where's Will? Is he being questioned by the FBI? By Travis and Zeke? I hope he's not behind bars. It occurs to me that maybe I should start to find him a lawyer when I hear his voice down the hall.

I jump from my seat. Travis and Will emerge from the back hallway.

"Lucy." Travis frowns. "What are you doing here?"

Will catches my gaze and gives me a look that tells me "no."

No what?

No, don't say anything? No, don't do anything?"

I'm so confused. And nervous.

"Hi!" I sound like I've just sucked down a whole balloon full of helium. "What's going on? Why is the FBI still here?"

"You tell her," Will says to Travis.

"Last night, Archie Clements confessed to murdering Jefferson Pike. He's been singing like a canary to the feds for the past four hours. Giving up all kinds of details on their real estate con. He gave up the money too."

"But that makes no sense. He told me he didn't kill Jefferson."

Travis gives me a weary look. "Not that again. Lucy, admit it. You were wrong. Archie Clements lied to you."

I am not wrong. Am I?

"So, J.W. Quicksilver ... "

"Looks like we don't need him, after all. The judge called off the court order."

I heave a sigh. "That's great. Isn't it?"

"It's great for J.W. Quicksilver," says Travis. "He's off the hook for Pike's murder, and he's still anonymous."

"What does this all mean?"

"It means that after the feds finish talking with Archie, we'll officially charge him for Jefferson Pike's murder. But it looks like it's going to be a long Saturday." He turns to Will, and the two men shake hands. "See you later, Cunningham." He nods at me. "Lucy." Then he winks at Paco and disappears down the hallway.

"Wow," I mouth to Will. "What just happened?"

"Crazy, huh?" He glances over at Cindy, who's watching us. She immediately goes back to her typing.

"Let's go outside," Will says.

Once we're in the parking lot, he tells me the rest of the story. "I got here around eleven, but I couldn't get in to see Travis or Zeke on account of everyone was involved with Archie's confession. Turns out, I never had to tell them who I was. Now that they have their killer, they couldn't care less about J.W. Quicksilver."

I shake my head. Crazy doesn't begin to describe the last couple of days.

"What are you going to do now?" I ask. "Are you going to stay anonymous? Or are you going to tell everyone who you are?"

"I don't know. What do you think I should do, Lucy?"

"Oh, no. Don't put that on me. You do what you think is right."

Then I think about it a minute. My best friend needs my advice. So I should give it to him.

"Listen, Will, you don't owe anyone anything. You have every right to keep a pen name. Jefferson Pike was wrong when he said you were asking to be scammed. In every way that counts, you were just as much a victim of Jefferson Pike as any of those people whose money he took. Don't let him suck the creative juice out of you. Keep being J.W.

Quicksilver if that's what it takes to keep writing those awesome books of yours."

He grins. "Gosh, Lucy, I'm getting choked up."

I playfully punch him in the shoulder.

"How about I buy you lunch?" he says.

"How about a raincheck?" I look at my watch. It's two thirty. "I have to go show Betty Jean how to clean up after a shift."

"Good luck with that."

"Dinner tomorrow night at my parents'?"

"Where else would I be on Sunday night?"

Paco and I get in the car, and we head back to The Bistro.

Archie Clements confessed to Jefferson Pike's murder. *Only I know he's lying.*

It makes no sense. Why would he confess to something he didn't do?

I try to reason it out like a puzzle. Did he have motive? Yes. Jefferson and he argued about the publishing scam. Archie isn't violent, but everyone has their breaking point.

Did he have opportunity? No. He was in a car trying to get away as fast as he could. He and Anita left the beach house at what ... four fifteen? Jefferson was murdered sometime between five and five thirty, about an hour after Archie and Anita had already left town. They were all the way to Tallahassee when they ...

They were all the way to Tallahassee?

Wait. What did Travis tell me again?

I thought you'd like to know that about an hour ago we caught Hoyt Daniels and Anita Tremble. They were outside of Tallahassee when they got stopped by the highway patrol for a broken taillight.

Travis gave me that information at almost ten o'clock the night of the murder. Tallahassee is less than a three-hour drive. If Archie and Anita really did hightail it out of town when they said they did, then by 9 p.m. they should have been almost to Jacksonville.

Which means they didn't leave town at four fifteen.

Anita and I got back to the beach house around four that afternoon. Once we knew we'd been compromised, we packed up and left the beach house immediately.

Archie said they left the beach house at four fifteen. He never said they left town. I made that assumption on my own. Which means he was still in town when Jefferson was killed.

There was something else about that conversation with Archie that has me puzzled. What was it?

I pull my VW bug into The Bistro parking lot. Betty Jean must be wondering what's taking me so long. I unclip Paco's leash and open the kitchen door.

Archie was disturbed when I told him that Jefferson never went to The Harbor House to see the potential mark, who I now know was Betty Jean. And he had no idea that Jefferson was murdered between five and five thirty. I gave him all that information when I went to see him at the jail.

Once again, I ask myself, why would he confess to a murder he clearly didn't commit?

And then, it hits me.

Archie was disturbed because it was in that moment when I un-wittingly gave him the missing pieces to the puzzle, that he was able to figure out who killed Jefferson Pike. There's only one person Archie cares enough about to take the fall on a murder rap.

Paco starts to growl.

The kitchen is eerily quiet. "Betty Jean?" I call out.

I fumble for my cell phone. I need to dial 911.

"Put that phone down, Lucy." Anita Tremble's voice sounds any-thing but mousy right now. "Or your geriatric friend here is going to get a free neck job." Anita is standing in the doorway that leads to the dining area. She's got one hand wrapped around Betty's Jean's waist and in the other hand, she's holding a paring knife to her throat.

Rats. I should have seen this coming. When will I ever learn? Will isn't the only one who suffers from too-stupid-to-live syndrome.

Chapter Nineteen

FORTUNATELY, OR UNFORTUNATELY, THIS isn't my first one-on-one with a crazy person threatening someone with a knife. If my past experiences have taught me anything, it's that I have to defuse this situation logically, without emotion. I need to reason with her. It's the only way I can get her to do what I want.

"Anita, you'll never get away with this. Now, please, before this gets worse for you, put that knife down," I say firmly.

"Make me."

That didn't go well.

"I'm only going to say this one more time," says Anita. "Get rid of the phone. Better yet, step on it."

"You want me to step on my phone? Are you crazy? This is an iPhone 11. Do you know how much this thing cost?"

"I don't care if it's made of gold. I'm not going to have you call the cops. Either you smash it now, or Betty Boop gets some much-needed plastic surgery."

"Hey!" says Betty Jean. "People say I look great for my age."

Anita snickers. "Shut up, you dumb cow. You looked ridiculous in that blonde wig, by the way."

Since logic and reason don't seem to be working, it looks as if I'll have to humor her while I find a way out of this mess. "Okay. Sure. No problem. I'll smash my phone. Just give me a minute."

"Now."

I blindly fumble with the screen for a moment and discreetly text 911, only since I can't see what I'm doing, I'm not sure if I was successful. I throw my phone across the room. It shatters into two pieces against the hard tile floor. There went my free upgrade.

Paco looks up at me like he's asking me what to do. I give a little shake of my head *no. Stay right where you are, boy*.

"Happy now?" I ask Anita.

"I will be as soon as I do what I came here for."

I'm afraid to ask what that is, but I think I have a pretty good idea.

"I don't understand," says Betty Jean. "What did I ever do to you?"

"Yeah," I say, "I don't get it. Why did you kill Jefferson? If Archie did it, I'd understand. They were partners, and money does crazy things to people. But you weren't even part of the gang until just a few months ago."

"You think I killed Jefferson over *money*? That shows what you know."

"Do you know that Archie confessed to the murder? He could have gotten a reduced sentence. Now he's given up the money and his life. For you."

"*What*? I never asked him to do that. You're lying. Why would he confess to something he didn't do?"

"Call your lawyer. He'll tell you. Archie confessed to the feds to save you. Because you're his daughter."

"You know about that?" Anita's voice cracks. "We could have had it all. The money, a great life. Until *she* ruined it." She tightens her hold on Betty Jean.

"Me?" squeaks Betty Jean.

"You had to have J.W. Quicksilver at your book club meeting, didn't you?" sneers Anita. "Jefferson was obsessed with Quicksilver's books. He must have read Assassin's Creed twelve times. After Archie and I found one another, he told Jefferson he was done with the real estate scam. They were going to retire. The three of us were on our way to Key West and then eventually the Cayman Islands when Jefferson saw this bitch's message on some reader board."

"And he couldn't resist playing J.W. Quicksilver?" I ask.

"He said it would be a quick thirty or forty grand. But it wasn't the money he was after. It was the opportunity to play out some stupid fantasy. To be the big author. You saw him that night at the restaurant? The way he signed books and flirted with all the women."

"You ... were in love with him?"

"In love with him? He was my husband."

"Uh-oh," Betty Jean mutters. "You mean ... I slept with a married man?"

"There didn't look to be much sleeping involved," says Anita. She laughs at the shock on my face. "What? You think that just because Jefferson was a few years older than me that our relationship was weird? It was love at first sight. For both us. Archie didn't approve, but it was a little too late for him to tell me what to do."

A *few* years older? Sounds like someone has some serious daddy issues. I think I'll keep that observation to myself, though.

"If everything was so great between the two of you, then why did he cheat on you?"

"Because he was a greedy S.O.B. who couldn't keep his paws to himself."

Travis was right. It was literally a crime of passion.

"When Jefferson told us that the real J.W. Quicksilver had confronted him, I begged him to leave town right away," continues Anita. "But he was having too much fun. He wanted to get his kicks and play famous author one more night. Archie and I left town, but I didn't want to go without Jefferson. We were about fifteen miles out when I convinced Archie to turn around and come back."

"So you went to The Harbor House?"

Anita nods. "By that time, it was around five, so we thought he'd be at the bar. When I realized he wasn't there, I had a pretty good idea where he'd gone."

"To Betty Jean's house?"

"She practically threw herself at my husband the night of the signing. It was obvious what she wanted. And he wanted to fulfill some sick groupie fantasy. So I snuck out a side door to the restaurant and walked to her house. When I got there, some old woman was peeking through the window. I waited until she was gone, and then I took a look myself."

"And then after Betty Jean left to go to the store, you went inside?"

She snorts. "She even did me the favor of leaving the door open. I wasn't going to kill him. But there he was, sleeping on that chair with this stupid *grin* on his face. She's eighty years old! What sort of sick age difference is that?"

"And you're twenty-five," says Betty Jean. "I hate to break it to you, but I'm a lot closer in age to your dearly departed husband than you were."

"Shut up! Or I'll—"

"Anita," I plead. "Don't do anything you're going to regret."

"It's too late. I killed my husband. And now she's going to pay too." There's a crazy look in her eyes that's making my palms sweat.

Who did I text 911 to? It could be any one of my contacts. But I really hope it's Travis. Or Will. Or even Brittany. At this point, I'd even take my mother.

Paco starts to whine like he wants to do something. But we're on the other side of the room. It's too far away for him to jump on Anita and surprise her. I could signal for him to slink over toward her. I know he'd understand. But I don't want to take a chance on him getting hurt. Besides, I really do think I can talk her down. I just have to find the right bait.

And then it hits me. I think I know her Achilles' Heel.

"Archie never suspected anything, did he? After you stabbed Jefferson, you walked back to The Harbor House, pretending to be inside the whole time. When you went out to the car, what did you say to him?"

"I ... I told him that I'd seen Jefferson and that he refused to come with us."

"So when he found out that Jefferson never met anyone at The Harbor House, he knew you'd lied to him. That's when he realized that you murdered Jefferson."

"I regretted that. Archie was good to me. I felt bad lying to him."

"Yet here you are, letting him take the fall for a murder you committed. It's not too late to do the right thing. Now that Archie has told the feds where the money is, he could get a light sentence. If he was cleared of the murder charges."

"You, on the other hand," shoots off Betty Jean, "will go away for life." The minute she says this, she realizes her mistake.

Oh boy. Just when I thought I might be getting somewhere. Betty Jean's big mouth is going to get us killed.

"You're right," says Anita. "I don't have anything to lose. You, on the other hand," she mimics Betty Jean's words, "are about to lose that wrinkled-up neck of yours."

The sound of a car pulling into the back lot startles Anita. "What's that?"

"It's the police," I say, hoping I'm telling the truth. "Right before I smashed my phone, I dialed 911."

"That's a *lie*." But the panicked look in her eye says that she might believe it.

"Do you want to take that chance? Put the knife down, Anita."

"No!" With the knife still at Betty Jean's throat, she forces her to walk forward. "You're going to open that door, and if the cops are really there, then you're going to tell them that I need a car with a full tank of gas. I'm taking this old bat as a hostage. And if you're bluffing, you'll be sorry."

Paco looks up at me as if to say, *I got this*.

For all our sakes, I hope he's right. But he's never let me down before. My Spidey sense tells me to trust him completely.

"You want me to open the door?"

"Are you hard of hearing? Yes. Open the door." She inches closer, still holding the paring knife at Betty Jean's throat, but now instead of being on the other side of the room, she's just a few feet away from us.

"Okay, here goes." At the same time I open the door, I look at my dog. He looks back at me. It's amazing how in tune we've become in the short time we've been together.

Anita shuffles Betty Jean forward. She's just about to reach the open door when Paco lunges and wraps his teeth around Anita's ankle causing her to drop the knife. At the same time, Betty Jean elbows Anita in the stomach. "Take that!" she cries.

I grab the knife off the floor.

Travis rushes through the door and quickly takes everything in. "What's going on?"

"Get this mutt off me!" screams Anita. Paco hangs on like he's never letting go. Good boy.

"Anita killed Jefferson Pike," I tell him. "She was about to kill Betty Jean with my paring knife. Archie Clements only confessed to save her. He's innocent. Of murder, anyway." But what I really want to say is, *I told you so*.

Now that the humans have a handle on the situation, Paco lets go of Anita's ankle and Travis cuffs her. Paco jumps into my arms and we hug. "Who's the best dog in the whole wide world?" I croon, scratching him behind the ears.

He barks as if to say, *Me*!

Betty Jean lets out a long breath. "Whew. For one hot minute, I thought I was a goner. Thank God you came," she says to Travis.

"I got a weird text from Lucy." He looks at me. "I tried to call but it went straight to voice mail."

"And you knew to come over?"

He shrugs. "Knowing you, it seemed the prudent thing to do."

Anita starts crying big fat crocodile tears. "This is a terrible misunderstanding. Please, Officer, I can explain." Oh, she's good. I can see why Cindy was fooled by her.

"You can tell us your version down at the police station," says Travis. I follow him out to the parking lot. He puts a still crying Anita in the squad car and promises to call me with an update.

Back in the kitchen, Betty Jean is calmly eating one of my double chocolate chip muffins. "I couldn't find whiskey," she says, "so chocolate will have to do."

I know exactly how she feels.

"Are you okay?" I ask her. "How's your neck?"

"I'm fine. But I think I'll spend tonight in my own house, thank you very much. Being your roommate could be hazardous to my health."

The next night is Sunday, which means dinner at the McGuffin household. The usual suspects are all here and accounted for. My brother passes the mashed potatoes while I give a recap of everything that went down.

"So Archie Clements was cleared of the murder, but he's going away for real estate fraud. Anita Tremble confessed to killing Jefferson Pike. I promised Victor Marino that I'd let Paco participate in a séance, and Betty Jean is sleeping in her own bed again." I also owe Rusty Newton free muffins for life, but since Travis is sitting across from me at the table, I refrain from adding that into the mix, because I really don't want to have to explain.

"Looks like everything in Whispering Bay is back to normal," says Dad. "For now."

Paco barks as if to say, *Don't expect it to stay that way for long.*

We all laugh.

"This certainly has been an exciting week," says Mom. "First we meet J.W. Quicksilver. Then he gets murdered, and then we find out he's not J.W. Quicksilver but some infamous con man. Then Betty Jean is almost killed by the man's wife." She shakes her head. "And then, in a bizarre twist of fate, we find out that the real J.W. Quicksilver was in town after all, but no one knows who he is!"

"Lucy knows," says Brittany. "At least, that's what she said. Right?"

Everyone turns to look at me. Even Will, who's looking at me the hardest.

"I was mistaken. I thought I knew, but it looks like I was tricked too."

There's a collective moan of disappointment.

"Well, not all's lost where that's concerned," says Sebastian. "I have some fascinating news. You tell them, Will."

Will lays down his napkin, then clears his throat. "It appears that Shirley Dombrowski is going to get a significant publishing deal."

"*What*?" I say. "Shirley? Sebastian's Shirley? How did that happen?"

Will looks around the table. "Shirley gave me her manuscript to read for a critique. Out of politeness, I thought I'd read the first couple of pages, but then I found that I couldn't put it down. It's quite brilliant, actually. I forwarded her manuscript to the same company that publishes J.W. Quicksilver's novels. According to his publisher, he read it too, and he agreed with me."

"All that in just two days?" Mom looks bewildered.

"I guess if you're a bigshot like J.W. Quicksilver, you can make things happen fast." I try hard not to grin at Will.

"Do you know that he's reimbursing everyone who came to the book reading the cost of their ticket?" says Brittany. "Not only that, but Betty Jean told me that his publisher is going to provide an advanced autographed copy of his next book to everyone in her book club."

"What a guy," says Dad.

"Do you think we'll ever know his real identity?" asks Mom.

"Probably not," I say. "You know those high-strung literary types."

Dad grunts. "Just as long as he keeps pumping out those books, I don't care if he's the man on the moon."

I notice that Travis has been unusually quiet. "I think Travis has some news, too," I say.

"Really?" says Mom. "What is it?"

I take a deep breath. "First, I need to confess something."

"Here?" Dad asks. "At the dinner table? Whatever happened to going behind closed doors?"

"I was never a member of Young Catholic Singles," I blurt. *There*. Now it's out in the open.

No one says anything for a few seconds. Then Mom shrugs. "I knew that."

"*What*? You did not. I totally had you fooled."

She raises a brow at me. Okay, I never had her fooled.

Huh.

"I have something else to confess too. Travis and I are only fake-dating. I said we were going out so that you wouldn't bug me about Young Catholic Singles."

"Lucy was fake-dating," says Travis. "I was dating for real."

I whip around to face him. "But now that you're going to join the FBI, it doesn't make sense to date for real."

"The FBI? Travis is joining the FBI? Does that mean you're going to move?" Mom looks crestfallen. I can practically see all her wedding plans for me crumbling in front of her face.

"I'm not joining the FBI," Travis says firmly. "That was Agent Billings's idea. Not mine." He looks at me. "I left Dallas to move to Whispering Bay to be near my dad. If I wanted big cop excitement, I would have stayed put."

"You're staying? For real?" *How do I feel about this?*

"Yep," he says. "And that's not all. It hasn't been announced yet, but Zeke Grant is stepping down as chief of police. Between Mimi's job as mayor and taking care of the two babies, they're overwhelmed. He's going to be a stay-at-home dad. And I've been offered his position."

"That's wonderful!" Mom claps her hands in glee. Looks like her imaginary wedding is back on.

"Now there's no reason for the two of you to not date for real," says Brittany. "Right?"

Travis pushes his chair back from the table. "If you all don't mind, I'd like to speak to Lucy alone."

"Mind?" Mom practically cackles with glee. "Yes! By all means, speak to her alone." She motions for Travis to sit back down. "You stay. We'll go." She nudges my dad's shoulder and starts barking off orders. "George, start clearing the table. Brittany, you and Will need to take out the garbage. Sebastian ... find something to do. Now." Everyone hops to do as they're told. Even Paco starts to get up.

"Not you," I say to my dog. "Anything you have to say to me you can say in front of Paco," I tell Travis. With a smug look on his face, Paco settles back down at my feet.

Travis waits until everyone has made their mad rush to the kitchen and the three of us are alone. "Have you had your talk with Cunningham yet?" he asks.

I could play coy and pretend I don't know what he's talking about, but why? "Will and I decided that we're better off as friends."

He nods. "Glad that's settled. So how about it? Want to go out next weekend?"

I pull out my new iPhone 11 (thank goodness I thought to get the first one insured) and open up my picture gallery to find the photo of Travis in drag. "First, tell me about this."

"Halloween party. I did it on a department dare." He grins sheepishly. "I was trying to channel Reba McEntire."

I laugh.

Travis waits for me to answer. He doesn't believe I'm a human lie detector or that Paco is a ghost whisperer, and for some reason I can't figure out, it appears that I can't lie to him anymore. He's annoying. Opinionated. And he sees everything in black and white. But he makes my breath catch. And he comes running when I text 824 to his cell phone (hey, that's what you get when you blind-text).

Maybe, just maybe, it might work out between us.

"Sure. Why not?"

Paco looks between us and wags his tail. I think he approves.

THE END

Books By Maggie March

Lucy McGuffin, Psychic Amateur Detective

Beach Blanket Homicide

Whack The Mole

Murder By Muffin

Stranger Danger

Two Seances and a Funeral

The Great Diamond Caper

Dead and Deader

Castaway Corpse

My Big Fat Cursed Wedding

Honeymoon Homicide Hijinks (coming soon!)

Want to know when I have a new book out?
Subscribe to my newsletter at www.maggiemarch.com for all
the news!

About Maggie

Maggie March writes page-turning cozy mysteries filled with humor, unexpected twists, and a little dash of romance. Born in Cuba, she was raised on Florida's space coast, and spent three decades as a labor and delivery nurse before pursuing her passion for writing full-time. She and her husband of thirty-seven years and their 2 little dogs live in central Florida, where she enjoys the beach, going out to lunch with friends, and solving challenging crossword puzzles. She's also on a lifelong quest to discover the ultimate key lime pie recipe (but not the kind they served on Dexter!). With three grown children and an adorable granddaughter, Maggie knows there is nothing better than spending quality time with loved ones.

Maggie loves hearing from her readers. You can write to her at maggie@maggiemarch.com

Maggie also writes heart-warming small-town contemporary romance as her alter ego Maria Geraci.

Acknowledgments

Most of all, I'd like to thank my readers. Without you, there would be no Lucy McGuffin or any of the other zany characters who live inside my head. Thank you for allowing me to pursue my wildest dreams as a published author!

I'd like to thank my copyeditor, fellow author, and friend—Chris Kridler, who tries to keep all my commas straight. Any errors, typos, or other miscellaneous literary no-no's are strictly on me.

Thank you to Kim Killion for my fun covers.

And last but not least, to my better half, my sweet hubby of over 35 years, who always believed in me even when I didn't believe in myself.

Made in the USA
Middletown, DE
09 August 2023

36441574R00111